"I believe it is customary to seal such a bargain," he murmured, and pulled her into a close embrace.

Color flamed in her face. His arms held her captive as his lips claimed hers, rousing old memories and old passions. Despite her father watching, despite her own reluctance, her body responded with a will of its own. Her eyes closed, and her hands caressed the broad expanse of his back as her lips willingly answered his. Desire flamed within her, burning away any remnants of decency and propriety. . . .

By Jeanne Carmichael
Published by Fawcett Books:

LORD OF THE MANOR
LADY SCOUNDREL
A BREATH OF SCANDAL
FOREVER YOURS

Books published by The Ballantine Publishing Group
are available at quantity discounts on bulk purchases
for premium, educational, fund-raising, and special
sales use. For details, please call 1-800-733-3000.

FOREVER YOURS

Jeanne Carmichael

FAWCETT CREST • NEW YORK

A Fawcett Crest Book
Published by Ballantine Books
Copyright © 1996 by Carol Quinto

Library of Congress Catalog Card Number: 95-90667

ISBN 0-449-22371-X

Manufactured in the United States of America

First Edition: January 1996

10 9 8 7 6 5 4 3 2 1

Dedicated to my sister,
LYNNE MULLANEY,
whose presence always makes
the sun shine brighter
and troubles seem smaller

Chapter 1

Miss Lydia Osborne reclined against several pillows in an enormous canopied bed that dominated her luxurious white bedchamber. She had decorated the room in the palest of blues and a deep, rich gold so that it complemented her blond beauty. However, this morning she found little satisfaction in either her surroundings or her looks. Her mind dwelled on the evening before. Although Sir George had written an ode comparing her long hair to the pale gold color of sun-dried wheat, and more than one gentleman had praised the vivid green of her eyes, she had felt strangely discontent.

Sipping her morning chocolate from a delicate Wedgwood china cup, Lydia sorted through a dozen or more hand-delivered invitations. None elicited more than a cursory glance before she cast them aside. After five Seasons in London, the last three as an acknowledged leader of the *ton*, Lydia admitted to herself that she was bored.

She mulled over the evening, trying to pin down what precisely had left her feeling irritable and out of sorts. She'd been sought after and feted by her usual bevy of admirers, despite the arrival of some very pretty young ladies in town for their first Season.

She had been introduced to a dozen girls, all sweetly anxious to please. She knew they courted her friendship on instructions from their mamas, for to be seen as an intimate of Miss Osborne was to ensure acceptance by the rest of the *ton*. The knowledge did not rankle—if anything, she felt flattered. What did bother her was the realization that three of the ladies she'd met were the *younger* sisters of girls Lydia had been presented with in her own first Season.

Miss Stapleton had conveyed her older sister's regards and the news that dear Phoebe was now the mother of two darling little boys. Miss Warwick confided that her sister, Abigail, had begged to be remembered to Miss Osborne and would have come to town herself were she not enceinte. The child, Miss Warwick had informed Lydia with a giggle, was due in July and her sister was already as big as a house.

Feeling suddenly old, Lydia reached up to run a slender finger over the smooth lines of her cheeks. Could she, at three-and-twenty, still compare favorably with young girls just out of the schoolroom? She was about to ring for her maid to fetch a looking glass when Finch stepped into the room.

An exceptionally tall redhead only a few years older than Lydia, Finch knew her worth. She carried herself with an air of assurance and frequently addressed her employer with an impertinence that would not be tolerated in a lesser servant. Dressed this morning in one of her mistress's cast-off gowns, which her talented fingers had refashioned, she immediately crossed to the long casement windows and drew open the curtains.

"Ah, 'tis a lovely day."

"Must you be so cheerful at this hour?" Lydia muttered. "And close those curtains. I am not ready to rise."

"I did not assume so, but you have a caller."

"Now? At ten in the morning? Have you lost your wits, Finch? Send whoever it is away."

"Oh, dear, are we feeling out of sorts this morning?"

"Not at all. I feel perfectly fine, or I did until you came in here aggravating me."

"Well, if you are not wishful of seeing Miss Lambert—"

"Perdita is here? You wretched beast, why did you not say so? Send her up at once."

2

Moments later a pretty, dark-haired young woman tapped on the door, then peeped in. "Finch said you will likely have my head for calling so early. Dare I enter?"

"Finch is getting beyond herself, and one of these days I shall give her the sack."

Miss Perdita Lambert laughed. "If you do, I shall employ her at once. No one has a way of doing hair like Finch, *and* she knows all the latest gossip."

"Oh, hush, and come tell me your news. I know it must be important to bring you out before noon."

Perdita fairly danced across the room. She deposited her cloak, reticule, and gloves on one of the tall wing chairs, then came to sit on the edge of the bed. Her unusually large brown eyes shimmered with excitement, and her normally pale complexion was tinged with a becoming pink. Happiness flowed out of her with the effervescence of champagne.

She reached for Lydia's hand and squeezed it. "Cedric proposed last night."

"Did he, now?" Lydia teased with a smile. "And to think I thought it was merely the pleasure of seeing me that put such a sparkle in your eyes."

Perdita rose from the bed and pirouetted twice. "I feel like . . . like dancing and singing and—is it not foolish—I cannot seem to stop smiling."

"Then don't," Lydia advised. "Am I to gather from this unseemly display of exuberance that you have accepted Mr. Richmond's offer?"

An impish grin curved Perdita's mouth as she nodded. "Without hesitation. Mama advised that when he offered I should not seem too eager, but I could not dissemble. Oh, Lydia, he looked so handsome and the things he said—" she broke off as a rosy blush deepened the color in her cheeks. Returning to sit on the bed, she reached again for Lydia's hand. "I wanted you to be the first to know."

"Thank you, my dear. Despite the hour, I am honored, and you know I wish you every happiness. How pleased your parents must be." Unconsciously her gaze drifted to the dressing table and the twin miniatures of her parents that greeted her each morning. Lydia knew her papa worried that she was not yet betrothed. He subjected her to an inquisition each time she went home, and this latest news would set him off again. But now was not the time to worry about that. She smiled at her friend. "Shall I ring for fresh chocolate to celebrate?"

"Thank you, but no. I am far too excited to eat or drink." Perdita hesitated, then added, "I really came to ask you to oblige me with a favor."

"You have only to ask," Lydia said promptly. Releasing Perdita's hand, she lifted her cup and observed her friend over the brim as she took a sip. The prospect of marriage to Cedric Richmond seemed to agree with Perdita. Lydia had not seen her this happy in years.

"Mama plans a ball at the end of the month to officially announce my betrothal."

"Naturally."

Perdita stood and took a few steps away from the bed. Her radiant smile disappeared, and she twisted her small hands together as she sought for words. "It would mean a lot to me to have you attend—we have been through so much together . . ."

"What nonsense is this?" Lydia asked. "Of course I shall be there. I would not miss your ball for the world."

"You may wish to reconsider when I tell you my news," Perdita said. Gathering her courage, she explained in a rush, "Justin arrived in town last night. Mama sent for him when she was certain Cedric would offer for me. He will stay until the ball."

Lydia's long lashes swept down, hiding her emotions, as she lifted her cup to her lips to gain time. Shock, surprise, anticipation, dread, all battled for dominance within her, but she had not spent five years in London without managing to conceal her thoughts. After a moment she set down her cup, and produced a credible smile. "Your mama must be pleased. Oh, Perdita, you

4

are such a goose. Did you truly think I would stay away from your betrothal ball merely because your brother will be in attendance?"

"Are you truly indifferent to him?" Perdita asked, coming back to the bed. She watched her friend closely. "I had thought—I mean you cared so much once, and you've turned down dozens of offers since—"

Lydia laughed. "Good heavens, have you been imagining that I am still enamored of Justin? How absurd. Why, when I met him we were still practically children. Oh, I admit I was infatuated. What girl fresh out of the schoolroom would not have been? He looked so incredibly handsome in his regimentals, and home on leave from the war—a true hero. Lord, I still remember how wonderfully romantic I thought him, but I would much prefer to forget how foolishly I behaved."

Perdita smiled, but doubt lingered in her eyes. "Are you certain, Lydia? Have you truly forgotten Justin? I remember how you cried—"

"Pray, do not remind me."

"I am sorry. Only I would not have you made uncomfortable or unhappy, and knowing how much you once loved him, I find it hard to believe that you no longer care for him at all."

Uncomfortable, Lydia snapped, "Why? I trust you are not still mourning John Mannerly." She regretted her words the instant she spoke and saw the flash of sorrow in her friend's eyes.

"Not mourning, no, but I shall never forget John," Perdita said soberly.

"Of course not, darling, and I deserve to be flayed for reminding you of him. This talk of Justin has stirred up all those old, sad memories that are best forgotten."

"They were not all sad," Perdita said wistfully. "We were extremely happy once."

"We were extremely young and foolish," Lydia said firmly. "Now, tell me that you forgive me, and then I want to hear exactly what your Cedric said to you."

* * *

After Perdita left, Lydia chastised herself for being seven kinds of a fool. She should never have mentioned Mannerly. Perdita had grieved deeply when John, trying out the paces of an unruly hunter, took a bad spill and broke his neck. They had been betrothed for less than a week. Lydia could still remember Perdita's white face and gulping, heartbreaking sobs when she'd heard the news. She was so crushed, so utterly unable to manage even the simplest of tasks, Lydia had insisted on going home to Cornwall with her even though it was the middle of their first Season.

A wretched year that had been, Lydia thought, remembering her own heartache. She drew a silk wrapper about her shoulders and crossed to the windows. Seventeen was such a dreadful age to fall in love. It took one so hard and never quite let go. Even after all this time she could still picture the way Justin Lambert had looked when she had first gazed into his blue-gray eyes.

It had been mid-January, just four days after she had turned seventeen.

The weather was bitterly cold that morning. Frost decorated the windows and the leaden, gloomy sky hinted at snow, but Lydia insisted on visiting her dearest friend, Perdita. The two girls were to be presented together in the spring and had much to discuss. As usual, her parents gave in to Lydia's pleas, and she drove the seven miles in the pony trap, with the promise to spend the night if snow came on.

She'd felt the cold dreadfully, her fingers growing numb beneath her gloves, and her eyes watering by the time she arrived at the Lamberts'. But she'd warmed up soon enough, settled snugly before the fire in Perdita's room on the third floor. Except for the maid bringing up numerous cups of hot chocolate and plates of biscuits, the young ladies had been left alone all afternoon, which suited them perfectly. They studied the fashion plates, planned their wardrobes, and giggled over a penny romance until a commotion belowstairs brought them out on the landing to investigate. Perdita heard one deep voice raised among the others and grabbed Lydia's hand.

"Oh, do come—it's Justin!" she cried, before rushing heedlessly down two steep flights of stairs. At the bottom, she catapulted herself into her brother's arms.

Lydia followed more slowly. Standing on the second step, watching the family reunion, she gazed directly into Justin's eyes—eyes the color of the winter sky when a storm threatened.

Justin stepped forward with Perdita still clinging to one arm, his other encased in a sling. "Hello, who have we here?"

"This is my friend, Lydia Osborne," Perdita said proudly. "I wrote you about her."

"Ah, the reigning belle of Kent," he said, laughter crinkling the corners of his eyes. His gaze swept over her as he bowed awkwardly. "I am honored to meet you, Miss Osborne."

Her mother said love at first sight was nonsense, but Lydia knew better. All it had taken was one glance—at least for her. And that was before she'd realized he was wounded and something of a hero, before she'd noticed how tall he was, or had time to note the strength of his jaw, or the generosity of his smile . . . before she'd felt the rich silkiness of his dark black hair that curled around her fingers . . . or heard the deep, resonant tones of his voice.

Five years last January, Lydia thought as she gazed out the window. Amazing that she could still remember how he had looked that day. She wondered if he had changed.

A tap on the door intruded on her thoughts. Lydia turned as Finch swept into the room with a deep green walking dress spread carefully over her arm.

"Well, now, I gather Miss Lambert managed to bring Mr. Richmond up to scratch. They're saying belowstairs that it's a good match," she commented as she hung the freshly pressed silk in Lydia's spacious wardrobe.

"He only proposed last night," Lydia said. "I am astonished at how exceedingly fast news travels in London, especially in the servants' quarters. One would think you must not have sufficient work to do."

"We talk while we work," Finch retorted, undaunted. "Would you like to know what they're saying about you?"

"Not in the least," Lydia said, crossing to her dressing table and picking up her brush.

"Let me do that," Finch commanded, taking the silver-backed brush from Lydia's hand. With gentle strokes, she started untangling the long, blond tresses. "There's talk that if you don't marry this Season, you won't marry at all."

With supreme effort, Lydia restrained her temper. She laughed lightly. "I hope you set the gossips straight."

The maid shrugged.

"Finch! Surely you do not subscribe to such nonsense? Why, if I wished, I could announce my betrothal tomorrow. The slightest hint of encouragement to any one of my suitors would be sufficient."

"Maybe yes, maybe no," Finch replied. "Having gentlemen dancing attendance on you when they know you've no intention of marrying is one thing—bringing 'em up to scratch is another. The truth is, some of the other maids have been needling me, asking what I'll be doing when you're on the shelf, and such."

"And what do you reply to such impertinent remarks?" Lydia demanded, a dangerous glint in her green eyes.

"Why, that my mistress will marry when she is ready and not a moment before."

"You should not be discussing me at all," Lydia said, only partly mollified. Still nettled at the thought of servants speculating on her spinsterish state, she added, "As it happens, I have made up my mind to wed this year."

"Have you now?" Finch asked, looking hopefully at Lydia in the looking glass. "The duke—now that would be grand—I can see me as lady's maid to a duchess.

Yes, Your Grace, no, Your Grace. I wager he employs more than a dozen footmen."

"Do not count your footmen before they hatch," Lydia warned. I have not decided definitely."

"What about that handsome Mr. Saunders? He'd be a catch with all that lovely money he inherited. Rich as Croesus, I heard, and you said yourself he dances divinely."

"Neither wealth nor the ability to comport one's self adequately on the dance floor are attributes I seek in a husband."

"They're not bad ones," Finch muttered, but not loud enough for her mistress to hear.

"The gentleman I marry must be kind, and possessed of a generous nature. He should be able to carry on an intelligent conversation, and share a sense of the absurd, though serious-minded when the occasion warrants. He should care about his estates, his responsibilities to his people, and his animals. Of course, I would prefer that he be pleasant to look at and dress with a modicum of good taste. And he must ride well, naturally."

"You're wanting a Corinthian, and to my mind, none of your suitors fits the bill. Take my advice and marry the duke or Sir George."

"When I wish your advice, I shall ask for it. In the meantime, you will please refrain from discussing my affairs in the servants' hall."

"Yes, Your Grace," Finch retorted mockingly and swept her a deep curtsy.

Lydia threw the hairbrush at her, but the maid dodged it easily and retreated to the hall.

Sir George Weymouth arrived promptly at four that afternoon, having previously engaged to drive Miss Lydia Osborne through the park. A tall young man, nearing his thirtieth year, he dressed with exquisite care and prided himself on his appearance.

After instructing his groom to walk the horses, he brushed a bit of dust off his buff pantaloons, assured himself his black Hessian boots retained their impressive gloss, adjusted the shoulders of his Bath superfine coat to make certain the padding was precisely in place, then strode to the door of No. 11, Bedford Square. The tall brick house was distinguished by intricately worked wrought-iron balconies against the first-floor windows and an elegant entry of Coade stone. He was about to lift the heavy knocker when the door opened.

Applewood, Lydia's aged butler, regarded him solemnly, his stout frame effectively blocking the hall.

"Afternoon, Applewood. Please inform Miss Osborne that I am here."

"Very good, sir. What name shall I say, sir?"

Sir George gritted his teeth. In his opinion, Applewood should have been pensioned off years ago. The old man never recognized him, though George was in the habit of calling on Lydia at least once or twice a week, and had done so for the past three years.

Knowing the butler's deafness made arguing useless, he withdrew one of his cards and pressed it in Applewood's hand. "Sir George," he announced, raising his voice. "Sir George Weymouth."

"Gracious, what is all the racket?" Sophia Remfrey asked, coming out of the drawing room. "Why, Sir George, how delightful to see you, and how splendid you look."

The gentleman breathed a sigh of relief at Miss Remfrey's appearance. His mother considered Lydia's aunt to be beneath notice, but he thought her quiet manner charming and rather restful, and could not understand why she had never married.

She was certainly attractive enough. Her thick chestnut hair fell in soft waves, providing the perfect frame for her heart-shaped face. Large gray eyes, thickly lashed, regarded one steadily from beneath dark, slightly arched brows, and she possessed a mouth that seemed always ready to stretch into a warm, welcoming smile.

George bowed over the tiny hand she extended and

remarked gallantly, "I must return the compliment, Miss Remfrey. Is that a new gown? The color is most becoming."

"Why, thank you, Sir George," she said, smoothing the graceful lines of the pomona green skirt. She had thought the style with the high waist and low-cut neckline rather daring, but Lydia had persuaded her otherwise, and it did seem to flatter her figure, which had become slightly plump with the advancing years. Blushing slightly, she smiled up at him. "If you approve, I know it must be quite unexceptional."

"Entirely in the best of taste, Miss Remfrey. How could you think otherwise?"

Her blush deepened and she avoided his eyes. "I fear I am getting too old for such youthful gowns."

"Balderdash! Why, you are a year younger than I—hardly an age one would consider old."

"For a gentleman, perhaps," she replied wistfully. Then, aware of how melancholy she must sound, she added, "But let us not speak of that. Will you come have a cup of tea with me? I do not believe Lydia is quite ready."

He laughed as he followed her to the drawing room. "I should be most surprised if she were. I took the precaution of ordering my groom to walk the horses in anticipation of a lengthy wait. But I do not mean to complain—not when I am provided with such pleasant company."

She poured his tea, remembering precisely how he liked it, and handed him the cup. "Have you heard the latest news? Cedric Richmond has offered for Perdita Lambert."

"So I heard, but that, my dear, is hardly news. The wagering in White's has been in Richmond's favor these last two months. The real *on-dit* is that Miss Lambert's brother, Lord Blackthorn, is in town. Have you met him?"

Sophia shook her head. "No, and that is very odd. I have known Perdita since I came to live with Lydia two

11

years ago, and I do not believe I ever heard her mention a brother."

"I am not surprised. He is rumored to be something of a recluse. Stays on his estate in the north somewhere and never comes to town—but surely you have heard of him?"

"Blackthorn? No, I do not believe so. Should I have done?"

"Justin Lambert, Major Lambert I should say, became quite a hero during the campaign in Spain. It was four or five years ago, but he was cited for conspicuous bravery. Saved a number of his men from certain death at the risk of his own neck. The Prince Regent was most impressed."

"He sounds a most courageous young man, but I never followed the news of the war. All that terrible fighting—" she broke off, shuddering delicately.

George patted her hand. "I know exactly how you feel my dear, and your sentiments do you credit. A brutal business, war, and this tendency on the part of the people to lionize soldiers—regrettable, most regrettable. But I fear we shall see more of it with Blackthorn's arrival. I have heard talk of little else this morning. Everyone is most anxious to meet him."

"Anxious to meet who?" Lydia inquired as she entered the drawing room.

George stood at once. There were occasions when Lydia seriously annoyed him, times when her behavior was such that he considered heeding his mother's advice and turning his attentions elsewhere. But there were other moments, like this afternoon, when she walked into a room looking as lovely as the sunrise over the Thames, and he was enchanted by her beauty all over again. Entranced, he stared at her.

"Anxious to meet who?" Lydia repeated, smiling sweetly at his befuddled state.

Sophia came to his rescue. "Lord Blackthorn. Sir George was just telling me that dear Perdita's brother is accounted a hero. But you must already be acquainted with him, my dear. Tell us, what is he like?"

Lydia shrugged as she drew on her gloves. "You must ask Perdita. I was introduced to him when he came home on leave once, but that was years ago. I doubt I would recognize him were we to meet now."

"You most likely will have the opportunity to find out," George said, crossing to her side. "According to the gossips, Lord Blackthorn plans to ride in the park today. Are you ready, my dear?"

She nodded, unable to speak. Her insides suddenly felt hollow, and her heart hammered loudly beneath the fitted bodice of her green silk. Whether it was dread at the thought of seeing Justin again or anticipation that caused the upheaval of her emotions, she disliked the unsettling effect. Taking a deep breath, she kissed her aunt, then allowed George to escort her to the door.

Too late, she thought, to draw back. For years, she had imagined this day, picturing scene after scene in which she saw Justin again—and walked away while he languished for love of her. She had lulled herself to sleep at night with dreams of meeting him at some ball, dazzling him with her beauty and exalted position in the *ton*, while he watched helplessly from a distance. She had pictured him bitterly regretting the day he'd turned his back on her. The dreams had comforted her at first, and then amused her—but dreams were a far cry from reality, and Justin Lambert was not likely to behave so obligingly.

As their carriage turned into the park, Lydia prayed that, for once, the gossips were wrong. But she knew the servants' grapevine in London was a network of un-erring accuracy. Even as she prayed, her eyes searched the bridle path for a sign of the tall, commanding figure she remembered so well.

Chapter 2

Sir George glanced at Lydia, knowing she was annoyed, but not quite certain why. The weather was exceptionally fine, and he had folded back the top of the carriage. To his mind, nothing could be more delightful than a slow drive through the park on a sunny afternoon, stopping every few minutes to speak to old friends and acquaintances. Others apparently agreed, for Hyde Park was unusually crowded. George, quite aware that having Lydia beside him lent him a certain prestige, relished the envious looks other gentlemen cast in his direction. But Lydia was not enjoying the drive.

To one who knew her less well, nothing might seem amiss. He, however, had known her for years, and when she was irritated, her eyebrows had a peculiar trick of flaring upward, angling away from her pretty eyes. The line was most pronounced this afternoon.

Sensing his regard, Lydia turned to him. "You are staring, George. Is my hat askew?" She reached a gloved hand up to adjust the deep green ostrich feather that curled becomingly over the brim of her hat.

"Not at all, my dear. Indeed, you look charming as always. I do believe you grow more lovely each year. Oh, I say, is that not Miss Piedmore?"

"Botheration," Lydia muttered even while she managed a smile and waved to the young lady in the approaching carriage.

"Shall I have Barrows drive on?"

"Good heavens, no, she would never forgive me," Lydia whispered.

George signaled the coachman to rein in, and greeted Cynthia Piedmore affably. She was rather short, slightly overweight, and inclined to wear gowns heavily adorned with ruffles and lace, which, unfortunately, did not at all suit her petite frame. Her lack of style might have relegated her to the fringes of the *ton*, but in addition to commanding a handsome fortune, she responded to the smallest overture with all the warmth and enthusiasm of a frisky, indiscriminating puppy.

This afternoon she was accompanied by Mr. Felix Neville, a young gentleman of good looks, impeccable lineage, and impoverished estates. It was well-known that he was hanging out for a rich wife, and the betting in White's was three to one that he would succeed in winning Miss Piedmore. Sir George and Lydia had their own private wager, she betting against the odds.

The talk between the couples was desultory for a few moments, touching on the pleasant weather, the unusual number of people driving in the park, and Lady Compton's musicale.

Miss Piedmore, in a misguided effort to please, smiled at Lydia. "Have you heard the latest *on-dit*, Miss Osborne? Lord Blackthorn is in town for the first time in years. I confess I had never heard of him until yesterday, but what a divine gentleman! We had the most delightful conversation—such wit he possesses, and not in the least condescending. One can readily believe the tales circulating about his heroic deeds."

"You would be wise not to believe everything you hear, Miss Piedmore," Lydia replied, a shade tartly. "I am certain the reports are much exaggerated."

Mr. Neville laughed. "I am obliged to hear you say so, Miss Osborne, for I was beginning to think that every lady in town was infatuated with this fellow Blackthorn. Makes it rather difficult for us ordinary chaps."

"Why, Mr. Neville!" Miss Piedmore scolded. "How can you say such a thing? I hope that a lady may admire a great soldier without being thought *infatuated*."

"Of course, my dear," Sir George said soothingly.

"But I quite understand what Neville means. Judging from the comments we have heard today, it does seem that Blackthorn has captivated every lady he has chanced to meet. And not one of them spoke of his heroic deeds."

"Precisely my point," Neville agreed. "If I heard it once, I heard it said a dozen times that Blackthorn possesses the brooding handsomeness of Byron—although Miss Pondsworth would have it that his lordship puts her in mind of Beau Brummell, such is his grace and style. And if that weren't enough, I can name you four young ladies who told me how dashing Blackthorn looks seated upon a horse. You will hardly credit it, Sir George, but one lady nearly swooned when she spoke of his air of romantic reserve."

"Why, I do believe you gentlemen are envious. Let us ask Miss Osborne what she thinks," Cynthia said, and turned to Lydia. "Have you met Lord Blackthorn? He was here earlier, but—"

"I have no desire to do so," Lydia interrupted. "It has been delightful to see you again, Miss Piedmore, but I think we must bid you good day. Sir George, there are a number of carriages waiting to pass."

Obedient to her wishes, George bid the couple a brief farewell, then gave his groom the signal to drive on. When they were in no danger of being overheard, he chuckled aloud. "Poor Neville. Would it not be sad if after all this time, he gets cut out of Miss Piedmore's affections by Lord Blackthorn?"

"My dear sir, I do wish you would not be so absurd. Lord Blackthorn would not look twice at Cynthia Piedmore."

"How can you be certain, my dear? She may not be a beauty, but she's a pleasant enough girl, and there is her fortune to consider."

Lydia put a hand up to her head, which was aching abominably. "May we please turn the conversation, George? I am aware that the town is frightfully dull this

16

Season, but surely there must be something worthy of discussion besides his lordship's return?"

"Why, certainly, but you know how the gossips are—I fear you must resign yourself to hearing a great deal more about his lordship—especially from Miss Piedmore."

Lydia bit her lip to keep from retorting that the lady had more hair than wit. No one of even the meanest intelligence could think Justin Lambert a clever conversationalist. As Lydia recalled, he was in the habit of issuing rather opinionated statements and expecting others to agree with him. She fumed remembering his high-handed manner and the way he had expected her to yield to his decisions.

"Lydia?"

She turned to find George gazing at her, concern mirrored in his kind brown eyes. Realizing belatedly that he'd asked her a question, she smiled ruefully. "I should not condemn Miss Piedmore's tiresome conversation when my own is so dreadfully lacking. Pray, forgive me, George, but I fear my mind was wandering. You were saying?"

He smiled, willing to forgive her much more than a moment's inattentiveness. "I only remarked that you appear to be a trifle out of sorts today. I do not wish to intrude, my dear, but if I can be of service to you in any way, I would consider it an honor."

"Thank you," she said softly, her green eyes glowing beneath the thick lashes.

Sir George inhaled sharply. He had never quite become accustomed to Lydia's beauty. When she smiled at him in that special way she had, his heart swelled with pride and he had the feeling he could move mountains—if she desired it. His mother's dire warnings that Lydia would not make a comfortable or dutiful wife were forgotten as he gazed into her eyes.

Even his own doubts, which frequently surfaced once he was away from her enchanting company, melted away, and all he could think of was how wonderful it would be to take her in his arms and kiss that luscious mouth. Casting caution to the wind, he began, "Lydia, my dear, we have come to know each other well these last few years. You must know that there is no one I admire more or hold in greater regard. If I were to speak of that most tender of all feelings—"

"How sweet of you, George, but look—there is Lieutenant Gregory," Lydia interrupted breathlessly. "Oh, pray, do stop the carriage. I *must* ask him about Lady Compton's musicale tomorrow evening."

The moment was lost, the mood destroyed. Obediently Sir George directed his driver to stop the carriage, uncertain whether to be annoyed or relieved.

The drawing room at No. 11 was considered small by most standards, but unquestionably elegant. Designed by the noted architect, Robert Adam, it was a long rectangular room, dominated by a pale blue Axminster carpet. Graceful gilt chairs and settees stood in inviting clusters near the enormous fireplace and in front of the mahogany bookcases, which lined one entire wall. Several large, ornate mirrors made the room seem bigger than it actually was, and reflected the deep patina of the rich woods and vases of fresh flowers that Sophia had placed at intervals throughout the room.

She looked around in approval. The fire was lit, the silver tea service stood invitingly on the center table, along with plates of the macaroons and lemon cake Sir George liked so much. The clock on the mantel chimed quarter past five. Satisfied that everything was in readiness, Sophia sat down to enjoy a cup of tea. She did not expect Lydia for another half hour, so she was surprised when the door opened and her niece walked in.

"You are returned early, my dear. Did you enjoy your drive?"

"Well enough, though the park was excessively crowded," Lydia replied, stripping off her gloves and tossing the cashmere shawl on a chair. "Is there any tea left?"

"Of course. I had Mildred bring in a tray just a few moments ago. I thought perhaps Sir George would come in with you," her aunt murmured with just the slightest hint of a question in her voice.

"He would have, had I asked him, but I put him off," Lydia said, cradling the delicate china cup in her hands. Though the afternoon was not noticeably cool, she felt chilled and drew her chair closer to the fireplace. Lost in thought, she stared at her cup for several moments, then looked up at her aunt. "Do you think Sir George and I would suit?"

A deep blush suffused Sophia's cheeks. She busied herself with the tea tray in order to avoid looking at her niece as she answered. "Sir George is . . . he is a wonderful gentleman, so kind, so thoughtful, I am sure any lady must consider herself most fortunate were she to name him husband."

Lydia nodded. What Sophia said was true, and yet she couldn't quite quell the feeling that accepting George's offer would be a terrible mistake. When he had nearly proposed in the park, panic had possessed her to the point where she had been almost rude in an effort to forestall him. That was a far cry from thinking herself "most fortunate."

"Has he offered, then?" Sophia asked quietly.

"What? Oh, no . . . no, not yet. I think he was about to, but I turned the conversation. To say the truth, I know not how to answer him."

Sophia shook her head and laughed lightly. "La, child, you amaze me. Had I your opportunity, I should not hesitate."

"I know I am being foolish," Lydia said with a sigh. "Such a match would certainly please my parents, but when I think of living in the same house with him, and seeing him every day—I vow the notion frightens me."

"Frightens you? What nonsense is this? Why, marriage is the natural destiny of any lady. What should alarm you is the idea of never wedding. I assure you, 'tis a state not to be envied."

19

The words were spoken lightly, but an underlying note of sincerity made Lydia glance at her curiously. She had never before questioned whether Sophy was happy. She had come to her two years before when Lydia's parents had agreed, reluctantly, to allow their daughter a house in London. They had suggested a distant cousin as a suitable chaperon and Lydia had agreed. Sophy Remfrey was not so much older that she could not enter into Lydia's feelings, and the two had become firm friends. Lydia had quickly given her the courtesy title of aunt, and was sincerely attached to her.

Sophy, always even-tempered and congenial, had seemed content with their arrangement, but now Lydia wondered if that were true. She hesitated, then asked, "Why did you never marry, then? You are so pretty, and amiable, I cannot imagine that you lacked for suitors."

"Thank you, my dear, but the sad truth is few gentlemen are willing to offer for a penniless girl. I fear I am doomed to the role of companion or chaperon." She smiled, but her voice quivered slightly when she added, "I only pray that my next situation will be as pleasant as this one has been."

"Aunt Sophy! Please do not speak as though you planned to leave me tomorrow. I cannot imagine how I would cope without you."

"You will do fine, Lydia. You are accustomed to managing your own household, and entertaining—I do little more than lend you countenance."

"You do a great deal more," Lydia protested. "And before I wed, I intend to make certain you are comfortably situated. Perhaps we can find a husband for you as well—that is, if it is indeed your wish to marry."

Sophia laughed. "I believe you have reversed our positions. It is I who should be looking about for a proper husband for you, my dear. Although in this instance, finding eligible and willing suitors is no onerous task— the problem is in persuading you to choose one among so many."

Lydia grinned. "Perhaps I should have a lottery. You

know, place all my suitors' names in a box and then draw the winning ticket?"

"Lydia! My dear, you must never say such a thing. I know you are only jesting, but if anyone else were to hear you, they would think you terribly conceited. A young woman in your position must be extremely careful—there are too many envious ladies in town who would be glad to see your popularity diminished."

Lydia rose and kissed her on the cheek. "See? I do need you to make me mind my manners. Without your restraining influence, I would probably tell Lady Cowpepper to go to the devil and George's mother what an appalling lack of taste she has, and then where would I be?"

Sophia glanced around to make certain none of the servants were in earshot, then smiled. "Be off with you, Lydia. You know you would never do anything so outrageous, no matter how tempting it might be."

"You would not be so certain if you'd seen Lady Weymouth's gown last night. Fortunately she is off to visit her sister for a few weeks, so I shall not be tempted. But honestly, Aunt Sophia, would you not think that a lady of her advanced years would have acquired enough wisdom by now to know better than to deck herself out like she was seventeen?"

"None of us wants to admit growing older, child, but yes, she should have better sense. If you marry Sir George, perhaps as her daughter, you will be able to gently persuade her to dress more appropriately."

"If I marry George, I shall endeavor to convince him to move as far away from his mama as possible," Lydia retorted with a laugh as she headed for the stairs. She just had time to change her dress before an early dinner. Later that evening, she and her aunt were attending the theater with a small party hosted by the Duke of Lansing, the second of her most persistent suitors.

In light of her decision to marry, Lydia studied Lionel Canfield, the fourth Duke of Lansing, closely that evening during the brief drive to Drury Lane. His Grace, at three-and-thirty was some ten years her senior, though he did not show his age, and possessed a youthful exuberance that made him seem much younger. He stood several inches taller than George, had wavy hair the color of fresh-cut wheat, a prominent nose, indecisive chin, and a wide mouth given easily to laughter.

Lydia had known him for several years, and generally enjoyed his company, for even his rudest critics conceded that the duke was the most congenial of fellows. Indeed, there was little to fault His Grace. He dressed well, having seemingly unlimited funds to spend on his wardrobe. This evening he wore a deep blue velvet frock coat, embellished with a high black satin collar and deep cuffs. The front was beautifully embroidered in a floral motif of gold, cream, green, and silver, and the same colors were picked up in his intricately worked waistcoat.

Brilliantly white lace showed at his throat and sleeves, and buff pantaloons, silk stockings, and black patent leather shoes with diamond buckles completed his ensemble. The expertly tailored clothes showed to advantage the duke's well-proportioned body, and Lydia thought there was probably not a more handsome man in all England.

Anyone, she decided, with even a modicum of taste must prefer the duke's patrician good looks to that of a certain rogue whose blue-gray eyes could burn with an unnerving intensity, and whose rugged features sometimes gave him the appearance of a rather harsh demeanor. And she was a lady of impeccable taste. Lydia gave His Grace her hand as she descended from the carriage and smiled at him approvingly.

If a pleasant appearance and agreeable nature were her only requisites for a husband, the Duke of Lansing would certainly be at the top of her list. In addition, though she did not know the extent of his fortune, she knew it was considerable, and His Grace was most generous. If only he were not quite so . . . so predictable in his conversation and habits.

"You look quite lovely this evening, Miss Osborne," the duke murmured as they entered the Royal Theatre and proceeded up the curving stairs to his private box.

"Thank you, Your Grace," she responded politely to the compliment, which was precisely what she had expected him to say. Lydia wondered if she was being too critical. But the duke had said exactly the same words, in exactly the same sincere tone, on dozens of occasions—as though it were something taught to him while he was in knee pants. His compliments never varied, never surprised or startled one. Involuntarily her thoughts flew to Lord Blackthorn and that faraway winter when Justin had courted her. He had told her once that she looked like a gypsy masquerading as a lady—passion-filled eyes and a mouth ripe for kissing were not the attributes of any well-bred young miss. On another occasion, he had compared her to a fallen angel; such, he claimed, was the purity of her beauty and the devilment in her heart.

Remembering, Lydia smiled wistfully. One never knew what to expect from Justin. Abruptly she recalled how he had left her—his regiment apparently more important than the love he professed to feel for her. Perhaps, after all, there was something to be said for predictability.

She allowed the duke to assist her to her seat at the front of his box, and through her lowered lashes, discreetly scanned the theater. Catcalls and whistles of approval erupted from the pit as she took her place and dozens of eyes turned in their direction to see whose arrival had occasioned such pandemonium.

She did look well tonight, Lydia thought, pleased with the reaction of the crowd. The roar of approval did not really mean much, for the gentlemen in the pit were a fickle bunch, but even Finch had commented on how well the new green satin gown suited her. Because of its simple but elegant lines, Lydia had chosen to wear her hair swept up in a cluster of curls, with her only jewelry the elaborately worked emerald necklace her papa had given her for her birthday last year. She knew the effect was one of innocent sophistication, and though it was vain of her, she hoped Lord Blackthorn might be somewhere in the audience, a witness to her arrival and the accolades she'd received.

Lydia lightly plied her fan and turned to address her aunt, seated on her right. "I vow half of London is here this evening. I cannot recall ever seeing the place so crowded."

"Edmund Kean is immensely popular," Sophia replied vaguely, her attention fixed on the stage where a one-act play was being enacted. She was one of the few in the audience to watch the performance, for the main feature on the playbill was the drama, which would follow. Most of the people present in the brightly lit boxes were there to be seen, and to see who else was in attendance.

Lydia turned to the young lady, a second or third cousin to the duke, seated on her left. "Do you enjoy the theater, Miss Gilbert?"

"Oh, yes, but we do not have much opportunity to attend unless Cousin Lionel takes us," the girl confided, and glanced behind her to where the duke was sitting. Her gaze was so worshipful, it was plain where her affections lay.

Her mother, seated on the other side of the girl, tapped her arm playfully with her fan. "Now, Nan, don't be giving Miss Osborne the wrong idea. Why, to hear you talk, one would think we were a couple of country bumpkins such as never goes to the theater, when nothing could be further from the truth."

The buxom woman leaned across her daughter and continued in a grating, overly loud voice, "Time, Miss Osborne, that is what we lack, as I am certain you understand. My dear Nan has received so many invitations since coming up to town, that 'tis difficult to choose

24

among them. Why, I declare, I get fatigued just thinking of all the parties we've been to."

Nan's embarrassed blush told a different story. Lydia rather liked the young girl with her red hair and freckled face, frank blue eyes, turned-up nose, and shy manner. Smiling warmly, she asked sympathetically, "Is it your first Season, then?"

"My first and my last, Papa says—"

"What my daughter means," Mrs. Gilbert interrupted hastily, "is that her papa is so certain she will take, we shall be celebrating her wedding by Season's end."

"Oh, I do hope so," the guileless Nan said. "Next year, it will be my sister Julie's turn, then Lizzie's, then Amelia's, and finally dear Caroline's."

"Gracious, you have a large family," Lydia replied, smothering a laugh. "Do you enjoy having so many sisters?"

Miss Gilbert nodded. "I miss them dreadfully. I am not accustomed to going to parties without one of my sisters in attendance. One always has someone to speak with, and Julie and I are much of a size, so we shared our wardrobes as well."

Mrs. Gilbert leaned over to admonish her daughter. "Nan, dearest, you must not bore Miss Osborne with all this talk of home—"

"I am not in the least bored," Lydia interrupted, then smiled again at Miss Gilbert. "Indeed, having no sisters of my own, I quite envy you."

"None?" Nan asked, astonished.

"Not one, though I do have a very dear friend who is like a sister to me. I shall have to introduce you, for I think you would quite like her. After an appointment at my dressmaker's, we plan to go shopping on the morrow. I could call for you, if you would care to join us?"

"I should like it above all things," Nan confessed, and turned eagerly to her mother.

To forestall Mrs. Gilbert accompanying them, Lydia leaned across Nan, saying, "Do allow your daughter to come. My aunt, Miss Remfrey, will be with us, and she is an excellent, and most strict, chaperon."

Had Sophia heard her, she would have laughed aloud at such a description, for she had long since given up trying to persuade Lydia to do anything she did not wish. Fortunately her aunt's attention was still focused on the play. Lydia arranged affairs to her satisfaction, then leaned back in her chair, quite prepared to enjoy the evening.

Behind her, she could hear the duke's low, melodious voice as he spoke to his friend, Lord Bathgate, and to the older man (Lydia had been introduced to as Mr. Fortescue,) who, she assumed, had provided the Gilbert ladies escort. She decided she rather liked the sound of the duke's voice. It was soothing—no drastic ups and downs, no towering rages or biting sarcasm. It was the sort of voice one could learn to live with.

Allowing the conversation to flow about her, Lydia relaxed and watched the players change the scenery for the first act of Shakespeare's *The Two Gentlemen of Verona*. There was some disturbance as Valentine and Proteus made their entrance on stage. Those in the pit jeered and tossed orange rinds at the actors, but after a few moments, the rowdies quieted down and a hush settled over the theater.

It was rudely broken by the late arrival of a party in a private box on the opposite side of the stage from where Lydia sat. Whistles, roars of approval, and a buzz of conversation greeted the tardy guests, so that Lydia, like the rest of the audience, glanced up curiously.

A woman clad entirely in white stood at the front of the box. She was not particularly tall, but carried herself with such an air that one had the impression of regal stature. As if aware of the audience's attention, she slowly allowed her pelisse, trimmed in white fur, to fall from her shoulders. Beneath it, a gown of white satin, embroidered with silver threads and sequins, shimmered in the candlelight as it hugged an obviously voluptuous figure, and displayed to perfection the lady's nearly

26

bare neck and shoulders. Diamonds glittered from her earlobes, in brilliant contrast to the waves of black curls that fell softly to her shoulders and encircled the slender neck lifted so proudly.

"Lady Castleletti," Sophia murmured, her voice rife with disapproval. "I wonder she dares appear in public wearing white so soon after her husband's death."

Lydia pretended not to hear or notice. She recognized the Baroness of Pembroke, of course—everyone in town knew the notorious, scandalous woman who had left her husband to live openly with another gentleman. She had not even the decency to marry the man after her husband had died six months ago—driven, many said, to an apoplectic attack by her outrageous conduct—but had further shocked London by replacing her lover with one handsome young man after another.

Lydia had heard the whispers that followed the baroness wherever she went. Curious now, she peeped beneath her lashes to see who had the dubious privilege of escorting Lady Castleletti. Lydia's heart stopped as her green eyes met the gentleman's deep blue-gray ones across the crowded room. Justin. Even after five years, there was no mistaking that fiery gaze—or the sardonic grin that curved his lips as he recognized her. She quickly averted her head and fanned her flushed cheeks.

Lewd comments flew. From the next box, she heard a gentleman say in a languid voice, "Ah, another handsome young man preparing to storm the castle's ramparts. Where does she get the energy?"

How could Justin behave so? Lydia fumed. Although she would be the first to concede that he had many faults—he was overbearing and arrogant, and too accustomed to having his own way—she never thought he would take up with someone like Castleletti. The man she knew may have scorned society's polite dictates, but he had, at least in the past, conducted himself with style and good taste. Was his arrival in town not sufficient to set the gossips on their heads? Did he have to

27

appear at Drury Lane with the most scandalous lady to grace London in years?

"Why, that's Lord Blackthorn," the duke said, leaning forward to confide in Lydia's ear.

"The gentleman with Lady Castleletti?" Sophia asked, astonished. "Well, good heavens!" She watched the couple for a moment, then whispered to her niece, "He looks nothing like dear Perdita—indeed, if I did not know him to be her brother, I would be inclined to think him the worst sort of rake."

"Perhaps it is the company he's keeping," Lydia muttered, then deliberately turned her attention to the stage. After all, it was no concern of hers. As the noise in the theater finally subsided, she tried to concentrate on the play. Unfortunately her wayward mind continued to think of Justin, and she imagined she could feel the heat of his burning gaze. Resolutely she kept her eyes fixed on the stage, determined not to give him the satisfaction of so much as glancing in his direction.

For once Shakespeare failed to enchant her, and the first act seemed interminably long. When it was finally over, Lydia turned to suggest to the duke that they leave early. But before she could speak, someone knocked on the door of the box. Mr. Fortescue excused himself to answer the summons, and returned a moment later with a folded billet in his hand.

"One of the orange girls," he explained, then smiled at Lydia in a jocular way. "The lass was instructed to deliver this to you, Miss Osborne, but she said no reply was expected. Sounds as though you have a secret admirer."

Surprised, Lydia accepted the note and unfolded it. She recognized the bold strokes of Justin's hand at once, and her cheeks flamed as she read the few scrawled lines.

"I have waited five years for you to come to your senses, my sweet, but my patience grows thin. Is it not time you admitted you were wrong?"

The gall of the man! The unmitigated audacity. Such

was her agitation that she stood, and had anything been at hand, she would have surely thrown it at Lord Blackthorn's arrogant head.

"Lydia, my dear, is something amiss?" His Grace asked, coming to his feet at once.

Abruptly aware of her surroundings, she swallowed her anger and managed a tolerable smile. "Why, nothing in the world, Your Grace, save that I find Mr. Kean's performance somewhat lackluster this evening, and suddenly I am ravenously hungry. Perhaps we should consider an early dinner?"

The duke was not at all averse to leaving, for he was not a fan of Shakespeare and had only chosen the play to please Miss Osborne. The other members of the party readily agreed and quietly followed His Grace and Miss Osborne from the box.

The duke's footman, posted in the corridor outside, was dispatched to summon the carriages. While the party waited, Lydia saw one of the orange girls leaning against the wall, and beckoned to her. "I am Miss Osborne. Are you the one who delivered a billet to me?"

"Yes, miss," the child replied.

She looked no more than fourteen and ready to flee if anyone said a harsh word to her. Smiling kindly, Lydia said, "I am merely curious. The gentleman who sent the note said no reply was expected?"

The waif shook her dark curly head. "He said as 'ow you would most likely leave once you'd read it. But if an you want, I could take him a message."

"Thank you, but no," Lydia replied, her pale brows angling upward. "There is nothing I wish to say to that particular gentleman—not now or ever."

Chapter 3

"Shall I see you at Juliet's this evening?" Perdita asked as she watched her friend try on a low-crowned, black top hat made of moleskin and trimmed with cock feathers.

"I suppose so," Lydia replied without enthusiasm. After studying her reflection, she adjusted the flat brim so that it sat at a jaunty angle.

"Oh, how pretty," Miss Gilbert cried as she and Sophia Remfrey came up behind Lydia's chair. She gestured toward the half-dozen bonnets surrounding her new friend. "But they all look lovely on you, Miss Osborne. However will you choose among them?"

Sophia laughed. "She will not have to, Miss Gilbert. If I know my niece, she will simply take them all."

"All?" Nan asked disbelievingly. She clutched in her arms a hatbox containing a charming confection of straw and satin, which she adored, although the price had been extremely steep. Left to her own judgment, she never would have purchased it. However, Madame and Miss Remfrey had persuaded her that the hat had been created just for someone of her size and coloring. Even so, she would not have yielded to temptation had not Cousin Lionel, on hearing of her expedition today, given her several pounds with instructions to buy herself a pretty bonnet. But to purchase six or more—such extravagance was beyond her comprehension, and she stared at Miss Osborne in awe.

Lydia, seeing the girl's shocked countenance, laughed. "My aunt is only teasing, Miss Gilbert. I do have a weakness for pretty hats, but I have no intention of buying all these—merely two," she said, gesturing for Madame to wrap up her choices. "And those are a necessity. Did you not see the article in this month's issue of *La Belle Assemblée* that stated that no fashionable lady would be seen in the same bonnet two days in a row?"

"Do not be alarmed," Perdita reassured Nan, who was looking somewhat daunted. "That precept only applies to ladies like Miss Osborne. You see, she is *very* fashionable, so others notice and comment on what she wears. The rest of us may make do with a good many fewer hats. And I have found that changing the ribbon or flowers on a bonnet sufficiently alters it so that most gentlemen would not notice if it is one worn before."

"I doubt most gentlemen would notice anyway," Sophia added. "Especially if a pretty face is beneath the bonnet. It is the women who notice." She sighed, a dreamy look in her eyes. "This reminds me of when I was a girl. Hats were so very important then, and I spent many an agreeable afternoon with a dear friend refurbishing ours. Young ladies do not seem to do that sort of thing these days, but we enjoyed ourselves immensely and created some very lovely hats, if I may be permitted to say so."

Nan smiled. "My sister Julie and I do much the same. I was thinking only yesterday that if I could only purchase some blue ostrich plumes—"

"Say no more," Perdita interrupted. "I know a mercer near Rosemary Lane who has every color and style of feather one could wish, not to mention ribbons and all manner of lace—and at a price one can afford. 'Tis not far from here. We could be there in a few moments, if you wish."

Nan hesitated, glancing at Lydia. She was Miss Osborne's guest, and it was Miss Osborne's carriage that Miss Lambert was proposing to commandeer.

Lydia, realizing the girl's dilemma, declared, "I think it a wonderful idea. We shall all go, and then one day next week, Aunt Sophy can instruct us on how best to alter our hats."

The matter satisfactorily decided, the ladies gathered up their reticules, shawls, and various purchases. Sophia accompanied Miss Gilbert to the door, leaving her other two charges to follow along behind.

"Do you really wish to go?" Perdita asked softly as she linked her arm in Lydia's. "I fear I put you in an impossible position. I am sorry, my dear, but I spoke without thinking."

"Silly. I have no objection—indeed, I believe it may even prove diverting. I am so tired of paying morning calls, going for endless drives, and seeing the same people year after year. 'Dita, do you remember when we first came to town, how exciting everything was, how eager we were to attend all the balls?"

Perdita nodded, but before she could reply, two ladies swept into the shop and claimed her attention.

"La, Miss Lambert, how perfectly delightful to encounter you here," Miss Fredericka Martin gushed, quite as though they were very old friends instead of mere acquaintances. "I was just saying to Claudia that we must call on you soon."

"And here you are, and looking exceptionally lovely, I must say," her companion Miss Severn added.

After a brief greeting, Lydia found herself in the unusual position of being virtually ignored as the two women vied for Perdita's attention. Amused, she stood aside and listened for a moment.

Miss Martin came directly to the point. "My dear, I understand your brother is in town. I do hope he intends a long visit?"

"He shall be here until the end of the month, at least," Perdita replied, looking helplessly past her to Lydia.

"Well, my dear, we must all do everything possible to make him feel welcome. Such a charming gentleman. Now, you are coming to my little rout party, Tuesday next, are you not?"

"A rout ... I really had not—"

"But you simply must come. Everyone will be there. And, naturally, Lord Blackthorn is welcome, too—I would not for the world have him feel neglected."

Perdita understood the situation at once, and answered coolly, "I cannot speak for my brother, Miss Martin. Justin tends to find his own amusements."

Claudia giggled. "He does, indeed. We saw him at the theater with Lady Castleletti. Really, my dear, you must wean him away from such company."

"I fear that task is beyond my powers. Oh, do pray excuse me—I see my friends are waiting." Perdita edged past them and, with her back to the ladies, wrinkled her nose in distaste.

"Remember, I shall expect to see you Tuesday," Miss Martin called after her.

"I vow, 'tis amazing how popular I have become since Justin arrived," Perdita muttered as she joined Lydia. "You would not credit the number of invitations I've received this week. I believe every female in town wishes to meet him."

"Well, you may acquit me of such motives," Lydia said with a light laugh.

"He asked about you," Perdita confided as they walked toward the carriage where Sophia and Nan waited. "I think he would like to see you."

"Perhaps, but I have no desire to follow in Lady Castleletti's footsteps. Really, Perdita, whatever possessed him to escort her, of all people, to the theater?"

She shrugged. "Her brother served in Justin's regiment and asked him to call on her. He said she was recently widowed and he was worried about her."

"Justin did more than call, Perdita. But then he always did have a passion for exceeding his duty. He should have stayed in the military."

Perdita sighed as they joined the others in the carriage. It was going to take more than a casual meeting to bring Lydia and Justin together again. They were so right for each other, but both were too stubborn to see how foolishly they were behaving. She wondered if Cedric might be persuaded to help her.

Several days passed in a flurry of engagements, and Lydia neither saw nor heard from Lord Blackthorn. His return to town was relegated to second place among the gossips by the scandalous behavior of the Prince Regent's brother, Edward, the Duke of Kent. His Grace had occasioned considerable talk when he installed his mistress, Julie de St. Laurent, at Castle Hill Lodge in Ealing, but now, supposedly in an effort to economize, for he owed in excess of a hundred thousand pounds, he had fled with the lady to Brussels.

Alexander Saunders, who had the dubious honor of once staying at Castle Hill, could speak of little else when he called to escort Lydia and Miss Remfrey to Lady Granville's ball on Friday evening.

In his mid-twenties and of only average height and unremarkable features, Mr. Saunders was among the most persistent of Lydia's suitors. It was not mere conceit that had led her to suggest she could bring the gentleman up to the mark when she chose. On several occasions, she had managed to ward off a declaration, for she deeply valued his friendship and held some vague hope that, given time, her affection for him might deepen into a more tender emotion.

He possessed two attributes that accounted for his popularity among the ladies. He was amazingly graceful on the dance floor and, as a rule, an amusing conversationalist. Of course, it also helped that he possessed a tidy fortune and was distantly related to royalty. The latter accounted for his visit to Castle Hill, which he was eager to relate.

He'd barely complimented the ladies on their appearance before introducing the topic, and it comprised the whole of his conversation during the drive to Cavendish Square and through the tedious wait of the receiving line.

Lydia thought that would be the end of it, but Felix

34

Neville greeted them as they entered the ballroom and almost at once inquired if they'd heard about the Duke of Kent.

"Decamping with Madame de St. Laurent, do you mean?" Alexander asked, looking a trifle smug. "There will be worse coming to light, mark my words. Why, if I were to tell you how he lived at Ealing, I daresay you would not believe me."

With relief, Lydia saw Perdita, escorted by Cedric, and smiled as the couple joined them. Her relief was short-lived, however, for after the flurry of greetings, Perdita turned to Alexander Saunders.

"I heard you speaking of the Duke of Kent. Tell me, sir, is it true that His Grace kept his staff on call twenty-four hours a day?"

"Indeed, yes, Miss Lambert. And no matter what hour one might arrive, six liveried servants would be waiting at the door. His Grace had an alarm system of bells affixed all along the drive to give warning, and at dusk, hundreds of lanterns illuminated the way."

"And if no one came?" Lydia asked.

"I beg your pardon?" Alexander asked, looking at her strangely.

"Suppose no one came," Lydia repeated, wondering if she were the only one to find the entire conversation absurd. "What did the six servants do then?"

"Why, I . . . I do not know, but I am certain His Grace had other tasks for them in that event. He was something of a martinet, you know. The last time I stayed at the lodge, I heard him give orders to the gardener that no leaf was to be left on the ground longer than fifteen minutes."

The others appeared suitably impressed, and Sophia urged him, "Tell them about the guest rooms."

Alexander nodded. "An eccentricity of his. His Grace has a passion for mechanical devices, and the entire house was crammed with clocks, model songbirds, musical boxes, organs with dancing horses—one truly has to see it to appreciate the oddity—and in the bedchambers—" he paused, shaking his head at the remembrance. Lowering his voice to just above a whisper, he continued, "Each room contained a door, which one would naturally think a water closet, but when opened, one saw the most amazing pastoral scene, done in miniature, of course, but complete with a running stream. I have never seen the like."

"I think it sounds enchanting," Perdita said, and turned to Cedric with a teasing smile. "Should you not like to have such a contrivance in our home?"

Richmond, a tall young man with sandy blond hair, had been in the military and still carried himself with the stiff posture of a soldier at attention. At first glance, he seemed rather stern, but when he looked at Perdita, his brown eyes softened and a smile erased the harsh lines about his mouth.

Though he laughed at her question, it was clear that Cedric Richmond would give his future bride the moon if she so desired it, and wrap it up in a silver bow. Watching the couple, Lydia felt a small pang of envy. Their's was a love match, and the affection they felt for each other was obvious ... she wondered if she could ever feel that way about anyone.

Immersed in her thoughts, she did not hear Alexander's reply, but the sound of the others laughing brought her wandering mind back to the conversation at hand, just as Cedric turned to ask her a question.

"Miss Lambert tells me you are from Maidstone, too, Miss Osborne. You must be acquainted with her brother, Lord Blackthorn?"

"I knew him several years ago," she replied coolly.

Perdita tried to head him off, but such was Cedric's enthusiasm for his ex-major, he never noticed her frown and said with a warm smile, "You must be pleased that he has at last come to town."

"Pleased?" Lydia questioned, her brows angling upward. Feigning boredom, she added, "I would not say so, sir. Indeed, the whereabouts of Lord Blackthorn are a matter of supreme indifference to me, and I am weary of all this talk of him. One would think he won the war single-handedly the way he is lionized."

Stunned, Cedric retorted, "He contributed a great deal to the effort, and in the process saved the lives of a dozen or more men. I know of no one more courageous or more worthy of being feted."

Lydia shrugged. "I am sure his conduct on the battlefield was everything admirable, but polite society is a very different milieu."

Perdita stepped between them. "Gracious, I believe Lady Granville is signaling to us to take our places for the first set. Mr. Saunders, are you leading Lydia out?"

"I have that honor," he replied, bowing gallantly.

Between Perdita's cajoling and Alexander Saunders's genuinely amiable nature, both Lydia and Cedric allowed the subject to drop and took their places for the opening minuet.

Lydia had no need to concentrate on the movements—she'd danced it so often, the steps were second nature to her. As she moved gracefully down the line, she considered her reaction to Cedric's innocent remark about Justin. She knew she had behaved childishly. She was still annoyed over the note Justin had the audacity to send her, and though she had not seen him since, she had heard of him from dozens of people—all of whom apparently thought he was wonderful.

That, of course, was no excuse for her incivility, and she resolved to control her temper. The next time someone mentioned Justin to her, she would smile and agree with whatever they said, no matter how absurd.

Her good resolve lasted through most of the evening, helped by the flattering attention she received from numerous gentlemen. Alexander Saunders was particularly attentive, and that arbiter of all fashion, Lord Rathbone, declared he had never seen her in better looks.

Lydia was pledged to stand up with Felix Neville for the quadrille, and they had just taken their places in the set when he stared over her shoulder, a look of astonishment on his face.

"By jove, 'tis Countess Lieven, and she has Lord Blackthorn with her!"

Lydia whirled around in time to see Justin entering the ballroom with the wife of the Russian ambassador. The lady had arrived in England a few years before, and instantly become the rage. Her thin, exotic beauty and continental sophistication had quickly set a new fashion. Members of the *haut ton* competed for her approval, but quickly learned to approach the countess warily. Though she could be amusing, she also possessed a deadly wit, and did not suffer fools gladly. Her smile of approval might mean instant acceptance by the *ton*, but her frown could just as easily make one a social outcast.

Lydia knew Countess Lieven well, and though she was disconcerted to see Justin with her, she was not entirely surprised. His dark, rugged good looks were exactly the sort that would appeal to the countess, who possessed a fondness for military men.

Remembering her resolve, Lydia turned back to Felix and managed a smile. "She always looks beautiful, does she not?"

He grinned and, in a low murmur, confided, "To say the truth, Countess Lieven makes me nervous. I never know what to say to her, but it don't look as though Lord Blackthorn has any problem. Did you see the way she was clinging to his arm?"

"I had not really noticed," Lydia replied, though the image seemed burned into her mind. She tried to dismiss Justin from her thoughts, but she had the uncomfortable feeling he was watching her. As the set concluded, she rose from a graceful curtsy, and saw that it was not entirely her imagination.

He stood only a few feet away, apparently engaged in conversation with Lord Granville, the countess still by his side. Trying to ignore him, Lydia lifted her chin in a haughty gesture of disdain, but she didn't miss the way his mouth twisted at the corner, a sign that he was secretly amused. In the past, she'd found that small gesture endearing, but tonight it only angered her. Was he daring to laugh at her?

Sir George came to claim her hand for the next dance, and Lydia managed, by an extreme effort of will, not to look back at Justin as she walked away. But she was still conscious of him and, at the first opportunity, stole a glance to see whom he had led out.

To her surprise, he was not dancing at all, but ensconced in an alcove, conversing with Cedric Richmond and two other young gentlemen she recognized as being "military mad." Despite his absorption in the discussion, Lydia was aware that Justin still watched her. She quickly looked away, gazing idly about the room. She saw Countess Lieven leaving the ballroom with Princess Esterhazy and Lady Granville—no doubt to discuss some hopeful's desire to be admitted to Almack's.

The ballroom was crowded. She saw Perdita in a set with Felix Neville. Cynthia Piedmore was dancing with Alexander, and Fredericka Martin had persuaded her brother to lead her out.

Executing a turn, Lydia smiled as she passed Miss Gilbert, dancing with Mr. Fortescue. She thought to make it a point to speak to the younger girl after the set. The Duke of Lansing had asked Lydia to do what she could for his little cousin—no difficult task, Lydia thought. Miss Gilbert was very sweet and not the sort to take advantage of their friendship.

"Rather a crowd tonight," George commented as their hands touched, and Lydia turned beneath the arch.

"Lady Granville's balls are always a success."

"I would say everyone who matters is here. Of course, none of the ladies can hold a candle to you, my dear."

"Thank you, George," she murmured as the set ended. She took his arm, intending to stroll toward the chairs at the far end of the room where Aunt Sophia sat with the other chaperons. She rather thought the next set was a waltz, and she'd promised to stand up for it with Captain Pierpoint.

Before she could reach her aunt, Lord Blackthorn stepped in front of her. "Evening, Sir George," he said casually, then smiled down at Lydia. "I believe this is my dance."

"You must be mistaken, my lord. I am promised to Captain Pierpoint for the next set."

"Ah, but rank has its privileges. He relinquished his place to me when I explained that we were such old friends."

Lydia, aware that a dozen curious eyes were turned in her direction, had two choices. She could refuse Justin, which would be a direct insult and stir up the gossips. And Sir George would undoubtedly feel it his duty to defend her from an unwanted suitor. He was already gazing at her, a question in his eyes.

Or she could dance with Lord Blackthorn and quietly tell him what she thought of high-handed, arrogant tactics.

Choosing the latter course, she reassured Sir George with a nod, then gave her hand to Justin. As he led her out, she smiled sweetly for the benefit of those watching, but hissed, "You realize, of course, that I am only standing up with you to spare Perdita the embarrassment of seeing her brother given the cut in front of half of London."

"I am delighted to hear you say so," he replied as he placed a strong hand firmly against her back. At her look of astonishment, he added, "There was a time when you would have thought of no one but yourself, but that you stopped to consider my sister's feelings when what you really wished to do was slap my face shows you have grown up. I have waited a long time for you to do so, Liddy."

"Do not call me that," she fumed, uncomfortably aware of the strength of his arm around her, and the enticing fragrance that was so essentially Justin.

"Too grown up for Liddy?" he asked, his mouth twisting in amusement. "What shall I call you, then, my sweet?"

"You, my lord, may address me as Miss Osborne," she said defiantly, staring up into his eyes. They were bluer than she recalled, and she couldn't help noticing the new lines etched around them, and along the corners of his firm mouth ... she remembered the last time she'd tasted those lips—and the exquisite sensations she'd felt from head to toe.

"Are you thinking of that night on the terrace?" he asked softly, his breath a whisper against her brow.

She denied it instantly, startled to realize he still had the power to read her thoughts. "Even if I were, no gentleman would mention such a thing. Your manners are worse than those of a stable boy."

"You will have years to improve them," he replied easily, then spun her around in a series of turns so that she was too breathless to answer.

For a heart-stopping moment, she was swept back in time, aware only of the hard, muscled strength of his arms beneath his impeccably tailored coat, the solid breadth of his shoulders, and the compelling deep blue of his eyes. It was as if they had never parted. Caught up in the magic, Lydia almost forgot her anger.

"That's my good girl," Justin murmured approvingly as he maneuvered them near the tall windows leading to the gardens. "Shall we forget all this foolishness and announce our engagement?"

Anger flared through her anew. Had he said he was sorry for once deserting her, had he even said he had missed her, she might have been tempted to reply softly. But Justin hadn't changed. The knowing tone of his voice, the amusement in his eyes, the sheer arrogance of the man was infuriating. Well, she would not respond like a puppy called to heel.

Lydia took a deep breath, endeavoring to mask the riot of emotions he stirred in her with a show of disinterest. "I believe, my lord, that you made your choice five years ago."

His mouth tightened the same instant as his arm.

"Are we to fight that battle again? You know that it was not choice, but duty that prevented our marriage. I had hoped that you had grown up enough to recognize the difference, but apparently not. My mistake."

The final note of the waltz played as he spoke. He released her and bowed, looking as unperturbed as though they'd merely been discussing the weather. "Thank you, Miss Osborne."

Aware that Perdita was quickly approaching with Cedric, and Alexander Saunders was right behind them, Lydia matched his smile with her own glittering one. But the sharp angle of her brows and the color tingeing her cheeks, belied the civility of her tone as she replied, "My pleasure, my lord."

Perdita shot her brother a look of reproach mingled with dismay, and turned to her friend. "Are you—"

"Gracious," Lydia interrupted, using her fan to cool her flaming cheeks, "the ballroom seems excessively stuffy this evening, do you not find it so?" Before Perdita could answer, Lydia turned to Saunders and laid a hand on his arm. "Alexander, do be a lamb and escort me outside. I believe I may swoon if I do not get a breath of fresh air."

"That sounds wonderful," Perdita said quickly. "Cedric and I will go with you."

Lydia turned back, her eyes unnaturally brilliant. "Stay where you are, 'Dita. I would not for the world deny Mr. Richmond the opportunity to speak with one whom he admires so greatly."

Perdita watched helplessly as Lydia walked away, then rounded on her brother. "For heaven's sake, what did you say to her?"

Justin did not reply until he'd watched Lydia disappear with Saunders. Then he looked down at his sister and smiled wryly. "Nothing, little one, at least nothing that she should take exception to."

Cedric, an embarrassed and unwilling witness, adjusted his cravat. "I cannot think Lord Blackthorn at fault. I do not know the lady well, of course, but it appears to me that Miss Osborne has an ungovernable temper."

"Well, she doesn't," Perdita snapped, turning on her betrothed with unaccustomed fury. "Lydia is the sweetest, dearest, most generous person I know, and I will not hear a word said against her."

Such was his astonishment, Cedric took a step backward. "I am sorry, my dear. I did not mean to, that is—"

"I think it best we retreat," Justin advised, placing a hand on the younger man's shoulder.

The moon was merely a slim crescent in the evening skies, providing only a sliver of light, but Lady Granville had placed dozens of lanterns among the shrubbery on the terrace so that it provided an enchanting place to stroll, and a welcome respite from the heated ballroom.

Lydia, however, was unaware of its charm, and walked briskly beside Alexander. She was thankful for the slight breeze that cooled her heated cheeks and did much to dampen her temper. By the time they had reached the far end of the terrace, which was darker and somewhat hidden from the vigilant chaperons' eyes, she was already regretting the impulse to leave the ballroom. Why should *she* be the one to leave? She turned to tell Alexander that she was ready to go back inside, but apparently he had other notions.

"Lydia, my dear, I have never seen you look more beautiful," he murmured, and boldly slipped his arm around her waist. "You put me in mind of a goddess, stepped down from heaven to enchant us mere mortals." He bent his head close to hers. "So sweet, so irresistible. . . ."

Realizing that in her anger she had stupidly allowed herself to be maneuvered into a secluded corner, Lydia tried to depress his sudden ardor by laughing lightly. "Very prettily said, Alexander, but—"

His lips choked off her words as his arms tightened

around her, pulling her close in a smothering embrace. For an instant, she stood still, curious to see if Alexander's kiss would arouse in her the same myriad emotions she'd felt when Justin had kissed her.

She felt his hot breath, and smelled an unpleasant aroma of tobacco mingled with spirits. His hand caressed her back while his lips moved wetly against her mouth. The only desire she experienced was one to escape.

Remaining perfectly still, Lydia refused to respond in any way. When at last Saunders lifted his head, she spoke calmly. "May we go inside now?"

At her cool tone, his hands instantly dropped away from her. "Lydia, my dear, I am sorry—for a moment, I was overcome by your beauty, by—"

"Do not apologize, sir. I am as much at fault for stepping outside with you." She turned as she spoke, and took a few paces toward the door.

He was beside her at once, apologizing profusely. "Say you are not angry with me," he pleaded. "You must know I meant no disrespect. I shall speak to your father at once—"

Lydia interrupted him, glancing up as she spoke. "I pray you will not do anything so rash, sir. Indeed, I believe it must be apparent we would not suit in the least, and I beg you to say no more—"

"Has our friendship these last two years meant so little to you?" he asked, reaching for her hand and holding her fast by his side. "I realize I cannot offer you a title, but you would find in me a devoted husband, more than willing to gratify your smallest whim."

"Please," she implored, making a futile gesture with her free hand. Belatedly she realized he'd had more to drink than wise, and his eyes burned feverishly. She tried to reason with him. "You must know such considerations would not weigh with me if my heart were truly engaged. Your *friendship* I must always treasure, but if I led you to believe I harbored more tender

44

sentiments . . . I am truly sorry, Alexander. Come, can we not remain friends?"

He gazed deeply into her eyes for a long moment, then raised the hand he held captive to his lips, and passionately kissed it.

"I trust I do not intrude, Miss Osborne," a deep voice said just behind her.

Lydia snatched her hand away and whirled around. "Lord Blackthorn! You . . . you took me unaware, sir."

"Obviously," he said. "I am loathe to interrupt such a charming tête-à-tête, but your aunt is looking for you, and cannot imagine where you may be. I suggest you allow me to escort you inside before the gossips begin to wonder as well."

"I will take you back to Miss Remfrey at once," Alexander immediately offered.

Lydia shook her head. "Thank you, but no. I must bid you good evening, sir." Her composure shattered, she docilely laid her hand on Justin's sleeve and allowed him to lead her away. As they neared the door, she said quietly, "I daresay you must think it very odd to come upon me with Mr. Saunders in that manner, but it is not what you are thinking."

"I doubt you have any notion of what my thoughts are at this moment—or would wish to know."

"Oh, you are the most disagreeable man I have ever had the misfortune to meet," she cried, her nerves completely undone.

"And you know so many," he replied, not in the least disturbed. "I will drive you and Miss Remfrey home. My carriage is waiting."

"What of Countess Lieven?"

"The ambassador has arrived and will see his wife home. I am quite at your service," he said mockingly as he held open the door for her.

Lydia saw little choice but to accept his offer. To ask anyone else to drive her home would give rise to the worst sort of gossip, and however little Alexander deserved her consideration this evening, he had been extraordinarily kind to her in the past. Nor was she entirely blameless.

Silently she allowed Justin to escort her to where her aunt waited with Sir George.

Chapter 4

It was, of course, impossible to keep a secret in London, and in the days following Lady Granville's ball, the news rapidly spread that Miss Osborne had left the premises under Lord Blackthorn's escort. Lydia refused to discuss the matter, and those few impertinent enough to inquire directly of Lord Blackthorn received a sharp set-down.

Given little to fuel the gossip, the incident might have passed into oblivion had not Alexander Saunders abruptly switched his allegiance from Miss Osborne to the heiress, Cynthia Piedmore.

Lydia thought little of it when she first heard the rumors. She had received an exquisite bouquet of roses from Alexander, along with a prettily worded apology, but had returned no answer. Although she believed she understood his reasons, and even owned herself partially at fault, she could no longer be on easy terms with him. Encountering him in the park a few days after the ball, she had greeted him civilly, but without that degree of intimacy that had previously marked their friendship. It was only to be expected that he would turn his attentions elsewhere.

The following day, when Alexander drove out with Miss Piedmore, rumors flew that he was ardently courting the lady. Lydia was surprised only by the choice of her successor. While Cynthia was kindhearted, amiable, and well-liked, not even her own doting mama would describe her as a beauty.

Then it came to light that Saunders had lost his entire

fortune on the Exchange. Unless he married for wealth, he would lose his heavily mortgaged estates in the north. Lydia was mortified anew. She had consoled herself after the ball with the reflection that Alexander had been carried away by passion. However reprehensible his behavior, she'd felt flattered to know she was so much desired. Even that small comfort was denied her now. The knowledge that he had no doubt acted from the lowest of motives left her spirits bruised and her self-esteem badly shaken.

It was in this melancholy mood that she received a very gratifying invitation to spend a week at Belvoir Castle with the Duke and Duchess of Rutland. She had met the duchess on several occasions, but this was the first invitation to visit Lydia had received, and the timing could not have been better. Nothing, she thought, would do more to improve her spirits than retiring from London for a week or so with a house party composed of the most select company.

Thus, a few days later, she packed her valises and journeyed north in a private chaise with her maid, Mary, and a footman to lend her countenance. Finch, laid low with a sore throat, had to be left at home, much to the dresser's disgust. In truth, Lydia missed her. Finch's acerbic comments on both society and scenery beguiled any journey, while Mary was still too new in her employ to feel enough at ease with her mistress to speak her mind. But the drive to Leicester was not a long one, and Lydia's first view of the castle was everything she could have wished for, sitting as it did on a rise above the treetops, and looking romantically splendid.

The duchess, all condescension, showed her personally about, introduced her to the other guests, and then left Lydia to choose her own amusements. She spent part of the afternoon attempting to sort out the names and faces of what seemed an extremely large house party. She knew several of the guests—Lord Rathbone, whom she was not at all surprised to see, as he was a great friend of the duchess, Lord and Lady Jersey, Lord

Alvanley of the Bow Window set, Admiral Tewes and his lovely young wife, Elizabeth, Miss Anne Channing and Mrs. Channing—but many of the others were new to her acquaintance.

She was presented to Frederick, the Duke of York, second eldest son of the king. She had not previously encountered him, as he had lived somewhat retired for several years after the Clarke scandal, when he'd been accused of selling commissions in the army through his mistress. Lydia had heard the stories, but on meeting him found them difficult to believe. Nearing fifty, the duke was rather stout, had a ruddy complexion, and twinkling blue eyes that clearly reflected his willingness to be amused.

She also met Mrs. and Miss Donaldson, whom she later learned were distantly connected to the duchess, which may have accounted for the younger lady's most superior attitude. Miss Donaldson, having made her come-out some years before Lydia, was unaware of the esteem with which Miss Osborne was regarded in town, and obviously thought her the merest nobody.

Lydia had been sitting with her in one of the drawing rooms, feeling increasingly depressed by the young lady's haughty manner, and wondering if she might not have done better to remain in town, when she looked up to see Lord Blackthorn escorted into the room by the duchess.

The sight of his handsome, familiar face in a roomful of mere acquaintances, made her temporarily forget her anger with him. As their eyes met, she unconsciously smiled. The earl made his way across the room, and as he neared, Miss Donaldson visibly preened, obviously thinking it was her own worthy self who had drawn Lord Blackthorn to their corner.

He greeted both ladies, then seated himself in a chair near Lydia and asked how she did. She had barely replied when Miss Donaldson put a question to him, batted her lashes in his direction, and appeared to hang upon his every word. Lydia watched, rather amused, as the lady used all the wiles at her command to hold his attention.

Justin did little to encourage the lady, but he did respond politely—to Lydia's considerable astonishment. Five years ago, he would have answered such sallies with a curtness that would have put a quick end to the conversation. She knew he had little patience with fulsome compliments and aimless chatter.

Fortunately before his patience wore thin, Lord Alvanley came to ask if Miss Donaldson would care to see a new bust just added to the Regent's gallery, and she went away with him.

Justin rose politely as the lady took her departure, but he resumed his seat a moment later, an amused look in his eyes. "Shall I go away, or do you think we may contrive to speak for a few moments without coming to dagger drawing?"

Still glad enough to see him in this strange company, she did not take offense, but smiled as she answered, "I cannot engage for you, my lord, though it does appear that your manners have much improved."

"I shook the straw from my hair before arriving," he said softly, the corners of his mouth turning up.

Lydia blushed slightly but met his eyes directly. "I will acknowledge I was wrong to say such a thing, if you will but own that I was greatly provoked."

"What? Because I wished to waltz with you?"

"No, my lord, but because of the way in which you went about it. A *gentleman* would have requested the pleasure of a dance, instead of arbitrarily taking it, leaving the lady little choice but to acquiesce."

His blue eyes, full of devilish merriment, mocked her. "And had I properly asked, would you have granted me a waltz?"

He was so confident, Lydia thought, so certain of his ultimate success, and with little wonder, for she knew few women who did not think him perfection. There might be new lines engraved on his brow, but they only emphasized the thickly lashed eyes, strong sweep of his jaw and firm chin. His boyish appeal had disappeared over the years, but the man was more handsome still.

She hesitated, then smiled. "How am I to answer you, my lord? The opportunity to be certain is lost. If I reply now that I would have acceded to your request, you will doubtless not believe me, or accuse me of being contrary. Yet, if I admit I might have refused, you will likely think yourself very right in arranging matters as you wished."

"Most diplomatically phrased, Miss Osborne," he replied, then chuckled. "I believe we are both much improved. Will you forgive my lapse of manners if I tell you I dared not risk your refusal because of the strength of my desire to waltz once again with you?"

"Very flattering, my lord. However, it was not your lapse of manners that angered me so much as your assumption, your rather arrogant assumption, that you had merely to return to town, and I would be waiting to fall into your arms."

The amusement fled his eyes, replaced by a look of graveness such as she had never seen on his face before. Lydia sat perfectly still, unsure how he would respond.

"Perhaps it was conceited of me to think the . . . attachment we once felt for each other would not have changed. Was I wrong, Liddy? Can you truly deny that we were meant for each other?"

She looked down, toying with the ivory sticks of her fan. How unfair of him to say such things, to look at her in such a way that she longed only to brush his hair off his brow, and ease the harsh lines from his brow.

"Liddy?"

"Please do not call me that, my lord. 'Twas a very pretty speech, but I cannot help wondering, sir, if you felt so strongly, why did you not seek me out in Bath, or come to town several years ago? In one who professes such deep and enduring sentiments, it must be thought odd that no effort was made by letter or visit to come to an understanding."

"Why as to that, my dear, I believe you know the answer. Had I come sooner, you would have handed me my head on a platter just to prove you meant your words. I had to wait for you to grow up, Liddy."

He rose as he spoke, bowing gallantly as Mrs. Channing and her eldest daughter approached. Lydia fumed silently even as she politely performed the introductions, all opportunity for private conversation lost. Justin would have the last word—for the moment.

After rehearsing various phrases to give Lord Blackthorn the set-down he so vastly needed, Lydia was disappointed to have no further conversation with him during the next two days. Dinners were long, drawn-out affairs, and she was situated halfway down the table from him. Afterward, he withdrew with several others to the card room, where they played whist until the small hours of the morning.

During the day, Justin disappeared with the duke and several other gentlemen who indulged their passion for hunting, leaving the ladies to amuse themselves with sewing, cards, the writing of letters, and long walks in the park with the few gentlemen who disdained hunting.

The company was pleasant, the surroundings luxurious, and under other circumstances, Lydia would have been well pleased with her situation. She had even won the admiration of Sir John Dinsmore, a young gentleman who spent his afternoons writing sonnets to the heavenly green of her eyes, or the perfection of what he termed her rosebud lips. His poetry was neither original nor well-written, but highly flattering all the same and balm to her spirits. Still, one could only endure so many sonnets before the novelty paled, and Lydia had received more than her share over the years.

On Friday, she woke bored and restless, determined to find some other means of entertainment. After breakfast, she conferred with the duchess, then took her sketchbook and her maid, and set off through the home park in search of the picturesque setting that her hostess had recommended.

She found a spot to her liking beneath a grove of trees at the foot of the hill, from which she could command a pleasing view of the castle. With Mary's help, she spread a cloth on the ground, then settled her skirts about her as she took up her sketchbook. She soon became engrossed in her drawing, and was hardly aware when her maid sought permission to stroll around a bit. Lydia nodded, cautioning the girl only not to stray too far, but her mind was intent on her sketch. Well satisfied with what she had done thus far, Lydia thought that if the drawing turned out well, she might present it to the duchess when she took her leave.

She worked contentedly for an hour or two, but her legs became cramped and at last she laid aside her book and rose to stretch. She realized she'd not seen Mary in some time, and the position of the sun indicated the afternoon light would soon be waning. Tentatively calling her maid, she ventured into the woods a little ways, but there was no sign of Mary.

Alarmed, Lydia began to search in earnest. Unlike Finch, her maid was a biddable girl, and anxious to please. She would not willingly desert her post and must either be hurt or lost. Lydia called more urgently, venturing farther into the woods, but no answering cry disturbed the quiet. Only the sounds of small animals rustling leaves as they scampered in the brush, and the raucous cries of birds protested her presence.

The light was quickly fading, both from the lateness of the hour and the clouds drawing across the sun. Lydia, realizing she would need help, reluctantly traced her way back to where she'd left her sketchbook, hoping that somehow her maid had returned. But when she emerged from the woods, there was still no sign of the girl. Leaving her sketchbook and blanket to mark the location, she hurried up to the castle.

The gentlemen had just returned from their day's hunting, and the drawing room was loud with their talk and boisterousness. Ignoring them, Lydia immediately sought out her hostess, seated on a gilded love seat near the great fireplace.

The duchess saw her approach, and greeted her with a smile. "Did you find a pleasant place to sketch, Miss Osborne? I feared the afternoon might be too cool. There seems to be a chill coming on in the air, but you may come sit here and warm yourself by the fire."

"Thank you, Your Grace, but I must go out again. I fear my maid has become lost or hurt in the woods, and I returned only to ask for assistance in searching for her."

Lydia heard a rude burst of laughter from two of the men, and Miss Donaldson looked down her long, thin nose. "How came you to be separated from your maid? It seems most odd to me."

Her mother added, "Doubtless the chit has wandered off and is enjoying herself with some woodsman. My advice is to put her from your mind. She will probably turn up later with some woeful tale."

Several of the other guests seemed in agreement, but the duchess saw Lydia's very real agitation, and rose at once. "Come with me, my dear, and we shall see what may be done."

Grateful, Lydia walked out with her and listened as the duchess ordered a number of footmen to begin combing the home woods, and a message was dispatched to the stables to set the grooms searching as well. Satisfied, Her Grace turned to her guest. "There, my dear, you may rest easy now. My people will find your maid in good time. 'Tis most distressing, I know, but perhaps a glass of sherry to soothe your nerves?"

Lydia shook her head. "Thank you, Your Grace, but I should like to go with your servants. I can show them where last I saw Mary, and perhaps save a great deal of time."

The duchess shrugged. Such concern over a mere maid was unusual. Servants were always wandering off, and comely girls in particular were invariably led astray by a handsome face. She'd had trouble with such girls in the past, and knew at least two gentlemen presently staying in the house who considered it better sport to tumble a maid than to indulge in an afternoon's hunting. But Miss Osborne was still young and no purpose would be served in reminding her of such things, or urging her to return to the drawing room. The duchess promised her every assistance, then took her leave.

Lydia hurried up to her bedchamber to fetch a cloak, and one for Mary, for as the duchess said, the afternoon was indeed turning cold. As she returned, she met Lord Blackthorn on the stairs, just coming up with Lord Alvanley, and was further delayed by explaining her mission.

Lord Alvanley, of the same persuasion as the duchess, advised her, "Dismiss the girl at once and engage another more reliable. A maid who runs off at the first opportunity is of little use. I don't tolerate such conduct in my servants."

"Nor do I, my lord, which is precisely why I am concerned. Mary is either hurt or lost, and I will not leave her in the woods alone. Pray, excuse me."

His brows rose, and he glanced at Lord Blackthorn in a manner that clearly said one could not depend upon the sense of any female. Infuriated, Lydia moved to step around them, but Justin stayed her.

"Give me a moment, Miss Osborne, and I will accompany you. No more than your maid should you set out alone."

She looked up into his face, expecting to see derision or the calm superiority she was accustomed to, but met only kindness and concern. Swallowing her anger, she nodded. "I shall wait for you at the foot of the stairs, but please hurry."

Whatever his failings in the past, Lydia came very close to completely forgiving Justin that afternoon. He behaved so much like a man of uncommon good sense, that had she not been overset with worry, she would have been quite in charity with him.

They searched for well over an hour before one of the grooms set up a cry. Mary had tumbled into a small ravine, striking her head on a rock, and twisting one leg beneath her. She'd lain unconscious for several hours, and when she'd finally come around, had tried to climb up the hill but found her knee would not support her weight. By the time Lydia arrived on the scene, Mary had been carried to the top of the ravine, and rested on a blanket one of the grooms had brought.

Her heart-shaped face was pinched by pain, dirtied from the fall and streaked with tears. Her plain muslin dress was torn in several places, and the girl seemed to shrink from the circle of men surrounding her. She greeted the arrival of her mistress with pathetic gratitude, clinging to Lydia's hand, and begging not to be left alone.

Justin, prepared for such a contingency, removed a pocket flask from his greatcoat, poured a generous amount of brandy into a tin cup, and then unobtrusively added a few drops of laudanum. He handed the cup to the girl, and bid her in a commanding voice to drink up. Lydia added her entreaties, assuring Mary it was just what the doctor would prescribe. The maid hesitated, took a tentative sip, coughed a little, but then drank the whole. She returned the cup with still shaking hands, but was able to give her mistress a wavering smile.

Dougal, Justin's own groom, stood at the rear of the circle and muttered loudly that it was nearly worth falling down a bloody ravine to get a taste of his lordship's smuggled brandy. Good-natured chuckling and joshing ensued, partly relief at finding the lass unharmed, and partly thankfulness that they'd not be out in the cold much longer.

While Lydia wrapped her maid in a warm cloak and rubbed the girl's chilled hands, Justin directed the construction of a makeshift litter from the blankets and a couple of tree limbs. Although two of the grooms had brought horses, he doubted if the girl could be persuaded to ride with any of the men. She acted as though she were frightened of the men, cowering back when any of the grooms drew too close. But he had seen Mary boldly flirting with more than one gentleman, and wondered now if her sudden shyness was not a pretense to enlist Lydia's sympathy.

Mary's knee was badly bruised and strained, but not broken, and by Monday she felt well enough to travel. Lydia made her regrets to the duchess, who expressed no surprise at their sudden leave-taking. If anything, Lydia thought Her Grace seemed rather relieved, though she said nothing beyond remarking that the girl might be more comfortable in her own home.

And safer, Lydia thought, but there was no point in complaining that her maid's accident had been entirely due to one of the gentlemen staying in the castle. Mary would not name the man, refused to even discuss it, beyond saying that "he" had crept up on her while she was picking flowers. Catching her unawares, he'd trapped her in his arms and ruthlessly kissed her. When he refused to listen to her protests or let her go, Mary had bit his lip, drawing blood. She shuddered as she told Lydia how he'd sprung away then, cursing something furious, and she had seized the opportunity to run away as fast as she could. She said "his lordship" had chased her, and it was because she was looking back over her shoulder as she ran that she'd not seen the ravine, and tumbled in.

Lydia had been furious, both that her maid had been accosted so rudely, and that the "gentleman," whoever he was, had been unfeeling enough to leave Mary in the ravine without seeking help. If her maid had cooperated, Lydia would have called the gentleman to book herself, but the girl begged her to leave it be, saying there was no harm done, and Her Grace wouldn't be appreciating no one stirring up trouble for one of her guests.

Lydia knew there was much truth in her maid's words, but the knowledge only served to fuel her temper. After church on Sunday, she had strolled on the grounds with Lord Blackthorn, wondering which of their fellow guests could have behaved in so reprehensible a manner.

Justin advised her to put the matter from her mind. "There is, after all, no great harm done."

"Is that what you believe, my lord?" she demanded, turning her frustration on him. "Just because my maid is not a member of the aristocracy, her feelings do not count? Suppose it had been I who was accosted? Would you still think no great harm done?"

The small muscle above his eye throbbed. "I would run through any man who dared to touch you. Does that satisfy you?"

"Indeed, 'tis gratifying, my lord, but because it was my maid and not I who was set upon, the matter must be set aside?"

Exasperated, he reached for her arm. "Not because she's a maid, Liddy, but because she refuses to name the man responsible, and because I am not entirely sure that she is blameless in this affair. What would you have me do? Challenge every gentleman here? Come, my dear, be reasonable."

She twisted out of his grasp. "Next, you will be telling me to grow up."

"Not a bad notion," he muttered, ill-advisedly.

"Oh, if only there was a gentleman here worthy of the name!"

He smiled at her passion. "I would gladly exchange places with any of your suitors at this moment, but however devoted they may be, I cannot imagine Alexander Saunders or the Duke of Lansing, or even Weymouth rushing to defend your maid's honor at the risk of his own life."

"Sir George would," Lydia declared, lifting her chin defiantly. At the derisive look on Justin's face, she stamped her foot and added, "He would if I were to ask it of him."

"Then more fool he. If you will but be sensible for a

moment, you will admit that your maid's feelings, which she will likely forget within a fortnight, are not worth fighting a duel over."

"By all that's wonderful, I am astonished to hear a gentleman feted for his military charges sound so nicely concerned over one small duel. Tell me, my lord, how many young men were you responsible for leading to their death in Spain? Did you calculate the cost in lives of each charge beforehand, figuring the Battle of Salamanca would be worth it if only four hundred soldiers died? Or did you fight so gloriously for a principle?"

The color drained from his face, and Lydia feared she had dared too far. She'd regretted the words instantly, knowing it was an unfair charge, but pride would not allow her to admit it.

After a moment Justin inclined his head. "Perhaps, if that is how you feel, you should seek out Sir George."

"Perhaps I shall, sir."

Miss Donaldson spotted them at that moment and came mincing over to beg Lord Blackthorn's opinion on some trivial point. Lydia, after acknowledging the lady coolly, deliberately turned away to speak with Mrs. Channing.

She did not see Justin again that afternoon or evening, save from a distance at the dinner table. Aware that he occasionally glanced in her direction, she conversed animatedly with both the gentlemen seated beside her. Feeling certain that the sound of her gay laughter must convince anyone that she was in the best of spirits, she resolutely ignored the tiny knot within the vicinity of her breast that persisted in regretting her altercation with Lord Blackthorn.

Chapter 5

Finch marched into Lydia's bedchamber several mornings later with shoulders held stiffly erect and a martial light in her eyes. She had not thought her recent illness sufficient to justify taking Mary Milton to Belvoir Castle in her stead, and had warned Miss Lydia that she would likely regret her decision. She had been proved right, of course; not that she was one to welcome a mishap merely to prove the worth of her own prophecies, but perhaps now Miss Lydia would listen to her.

After drawing back the curtains, Finch fussed noisily about the room, waiting until her mistress had drunk her morning cup of chocolate and sorted through the stack of various invitations before commenting, "That Mary is getting above herself, miss, and I fear you will have to speak with her."

"What is it now?" Lydia asked with a weary sigh.

"Far be it for me to come bearing tales, but for all her knee's too sore to allow her to do any work, her mouth is running fine. Going on and on, she is, about how this lord was so taken with her, he followed her into the woods at Belvoir. Wouldn't take no for an answer, and chased her until she fell into that ravine—"

"I know it distresses you, Finch, but it is true she was set upon."

Finch tossed her head back. "Lordy, Miss Lydia, as though any maid worth her salt hasn't been given the eye sometime or other by a gentleman. Why, if I was to tell you the number of times I've been approached—"

"You have told me, and I am quite willing to concede that had you been at Belvoir instead of Mary, you doubtless would have been chased in her place. I am only thankful you were not, for I cannot do without your services."

Somewhat mollified, the tall dresser sniffed. "That's as may be, miss, but I hope I know how to make it clear to a gentleman that I ain't free with my favors like some as I could name, and I hope I'd know better than to leave you sitting alone to go gamboling off in the woods by myself."

Lydia picked up her invitations again, listening with only half an ear to her maid's complaints. She'd heard much the same every morning since her return. Finch greatly resented Mary and the fuss that had been made over the girl. In truth, Lydia was beginning to feel much the same.

After cutting short her visit to Belvoir, and falling out with Lord Blackthorn over the wretched girl, the least Lydia had expected was for the maid to go into a decline. It was not that she wished Mary to suffer, but a show of maidenly reserve, some sign that the maid felt ill-used, would have done much to make Lydia feel she'd been justified in rushing to the girl's defense. Instead, once away from the castle, Mary had recovered amazingly fast, and they had not been home above an hour, before she was regaling most of the staff with a highly embellished version of her adventure.

Aunt Sophy, when informed of the reason for their early return, had been less than sympathetic. Lydia, feeling foolish, tried to explain how horribly Mary had been hurt, and how frightened she herself had been to find her maid injured and lying lifeless in a ravine. But Sophy had seen Mary laughing as two footmen assisted her into the house, and found it difficult to believe the girl had sustained any lasting injury. Indeed, were it not for the obvious swelling of Mary's knee, one would not think her hurt at all, which in truth Lydia found extremely annoying.

Nor did it soothe her feelings to hear Finch complaining every morning that the younger maid seemed to be enjoying herself as she recovered, or that Henry, the second footman, was neglecting his duties in order to spend as much time as possible with Mary.

"Mark my words," Finch warned. "That girl will soon be in trouble and bringing disgrace to this house."

"As I rather doubt she can do much before her knee heals, I suggest you quit worrying your head over her. If you are in need of distraction, I can think of any number of ways to better occupy your mind. My green silk has a tiny tear in the hem, and the ribbons on my blue walking dress are sadly frayed."

"I've already seen to that, miss," Finch informed her coolly, then muttered beneath her breath, "Though it's a wonder I had the time, what with having to do my work and *hers*, too." But one glance at her mistress's stormy countenance was sufficient to send her scurrying to the wardrobe without further protest.

Lydia knew she would have to do something about Mary in order to placate Finch. Her dresser had been with her for a number of years; not only was she a superior servant, but Lydia was genuinely fond of her.

However, dismissing Mary merely to please Finch was beyond consideration. Lydia still felt a measure of responsibility for the maid, and her own mother, Lady Claire, had highly recommended the girl, who was competent enough. To discharge her without reason would be dreadfully unfair, especially so since Lydia knew Mary sent a good portion of her wages home to Cornwall to help support a rather large number of brothers and sisters.

Perdita might be willing to engage the girl . . . but if she sent her there, Justin would likely encounter her, and Lydia shuddered as she imagined him inquiring about the girl's ordeal—and Mary's saucy answer. No, perhaps it was cowardly of her, but after their argument, she hoped he never learned just how swiftly her maid had recovered.

Lydia was still mulling over various acquaintances who might be persuaded to employ the girl when Sir George Weymouth called that evening. He was escorting her and Aunt Sophy to a musicale at Lady Fitzhugh's to hear the new diva, Anna Maria Pavaroti, perform. Lydia had agreed to the engagement because one did not refuse an invitation to Lady Fitzhugh's, and because she knew it would provide her aunt a great deal of enjoyment. Both Sophy and Sir George were devotees of the opera, and quite capable of spending hours debating the merits of Madam Pavaroti as opposed to Angelica Catalana.

Lydia listened to them arguing happily during the carriage drive, and again after the performance, while paying very little attention. Her mind occupied with other concerns, she pretended an interest she was far from feeling, and, when asked, professed a preference for Pavaroti. In truth, Lydia could discern no recognizable difference between the divas. She had discovered at a tender age that she was tone deaf, having overheard the music master describe her voice as an offense to nature, and her performance on the spinet as excruciatingly painful.

At the time, Lydia had been devastated, for she enjoyed nothing more when in spirits than to lift her voice in song. However, she sadly accepted the advice of her mother and thereafter confined her singing to those moments when she was entirely alone. Most people in London were unaware of the true reason why the elegant Miss Osborne could never be persuaded to perform at any gathering. The observant few set it down to a becoming modesty. Only Perdita knew the truth—Perdita and her brother.

She had nearly forgotten that long-ago afternoon when Justin had come upon her, taking her by surprise. It had been one of those glorious, rare days of summer when the meadows were lushly green, the sky a pure, sweet blue, and the warmth of the sun sufficient to melt the coldest heart.

Unable to sit quietly indoors on such a day, she'd ridden her mare out, racing over the fields, flying across impossible jumps, until both were nearly spent. They had stopped finally, she and Shadow, at the stream that crossed the northern part of the estate. After walking the mare to cool her, and allowing her to drink from the stream, Lydia had settled on a wide rock to bask in the sun.

Justin had proposed the evening before, and Lydia, reliving the moment, thought she would likely burst from the happiness that swelled inside her. She remembered the outrageous compliments he'd whispered in her ear, the delightful kisses he'd stolen in the courtyard, and the inexplicable yearnings he stirred in her heart.

Too happy not to, she had given voice to her joy, singing softly about a young girl who'd fallen in love with a dark-haired stranger—and she'd nearly fallen into the stream when Justin's deep, rich voice had suddenly joined hers. He had caught her easily enough, and drawn her to her feet.

She had stopped singing at once, of course. "I . . . I did not know anyone was about," she'd said, suddenly shy of him.

"Your mother told me where I might find you," Justin murmured, his lips brushing her brow. "But I think my heart would have led me to you. I could not stop thinking of you last night. Were you singing about me?"

Blushing uncontrollably, she'd declaimed, "I know I do not have any voice—"

"I think it charming."

"And I cannot carry a tune—"

"No one would notice, not when you look so beautiful you take my breath away."

Toying with the buttons on his coat, she'd confessed, "Mama thinks it best I do not sing at all."

His warm laugh rang out, and he hugged her to him. "Good. Then only I shall know how utterly delightful you are. You shall sing only for me. Now, kiss me, Liddy, quick, before I die from desire."

The memories came flooding back, along with the knowledge that Justin knew her secret, as he took her by surprise again. She had glanced up to find him suddenly looming over her chair, regarding her with a quizzical gleam in his blue eyes. Lydia masked the sinking feeling in the pit of her stomach with a brilliant smile and inquired how he did.

"Delightfully, Miss Osborne. Seldom have I enjoyed an evening more, but I own myself astonished to hear you say you prefer Madam Pavaroti to the great Catalana. Surely, there can be no comparison?"

Lydia glared at him.

Sir George shook his head. "I must beg to differ with you, Lord Blackthorn. Catalana may be the better known of the pair, but I think Miss Osborne in the right of it; Pavaroti has the greater range."

"Of course," Justin murmured, looking from Weymouth to Lydia. "Miss Osborne would undoubtedly know."

"Well, I do not agree," the young blonde clinging to Blackthorn's arm declared. Gazing at Justin worshipfully, she purred, "I think *you* are right, my lord. Catalana is the better of the two."

Lydia, resisting a strong urge to advise the girl not to be quite so obvious, smiled sweetly. "And have you heard Catalana perform, Miss Stapleton?"

"Well, no, but I hope to have the opportunity soon," she replied, and turned her large eyes pointedly in Justin's direction.

Lydia had to admit he was looking particularly handsome in a well-fitting blue frock coat, no doubt cut by Weston if one judged by the simplicity of the lines. His stock, of snow white linen, was perfectly but simply tied above moderately starched shirt points, and his waistcoat, though heavily embroidered with blue silk, was modest by most standards. Even his hair, which she knew had a tendency to fall in disordered waves across his brow, was brushed neatly back—but was that any reason for Miss Stapleton to behave in such a besotted manner?

Justin did not rise to the bait, but solicitously seated Miss Stapleton, suggesting she might care to rest her pretty little feet. The girl simpered, primly sat down next to Sophia Remfrey on the gilded settee, and carelessly allowed her cashmere shawl to fall off her shoulders. The gentlemen standing had a very clear view of the young lady's extremely low-cut bodice, and the abundance displayed therein.

Unable to watch such shameless posturing, Lydia turned to George, waving her fan languidly. "Gracious, but Lady Fitzhugh keeps her rooms exceptionally warm. I do not know how Pavaroti managed to sing at all, for I vow my own throat is quite parched."

Sir George at once volunteered to fetch her a glass of champagne, inquired if the other ladies desired a drink, then hurried off.

While Sophia attempted to engage Miss Stapleton in conversation, Justin strolled behind the sofa until he stood near Lydia's chair, leaned over, and murmured softly, "How well trained Weymouth is. He shall make some woman an admirable husband."

"If by that you mean to imply that he is thoughtful and considerate, then I must agree, my lord."

"I rather thought you would. Of course he will have small chance of a wedding unless you let him off the leash sufficiently long to find a bride. 'Tis unkind of you, Liddy, to keep him at heel when you have no intention of marrying him."

Lydia bristled and, through gritted teeth, hissed, "You can have no notion of what I intend, but I would not advise you to wager against such an outcome."

"But, my dear, they are giving three to one in White's that you shall bring him up to scratch before the Season ends. Difficult to resist such odds."

"Wager, then, if you are of a mind to lose heavily."

He flicked her cheek with a gloved finger. "You will never wed him, Liddy, that much I promise you."

Perdita, strolling up to the group with Cedric Richmond, took one glance at the fury in her friend's eyes and the amused countenance of her brother, and hastily intervened. "Justin, my dear, Lady Fitzhugh desires a word with you. I believe she wishes to hear your opinion of Madam Pavaroti's performance."

"Does she? How very odd—I spoke with her just a few moments ago."

Cedric looked with considerable surprise at Perdita. "I did not hear Lady Fitzhugh say—"

"You were not listening," she interrupted, pinching his arm in warning. "Oh, Sir George, good evening, sir. Did you enjoy the performance?"

He nodded while carefully handing Lydia and Sophia their drinks. "I did indeed, Miss Lambert." He went on speaking with much enthusiasm about the diva, but only Sophia paid any real attention.

Miss Stapleton barely concealed a yawn behind her fan, then beckoned to Lord Blackthorn. "I believe I saw Miss Cleveland earlier, and I really must speak with her. Would you be so good as to give me your escort, my lord?"

"I am entirely at your service," Justin replied, bowing gallantly before offering his arm.

Perdita, watching them walk away, muttered, "Little cat. Sometimes I wonder if Justin has taken leave of his senses. He could have escorted any one of a dozen ladies here this evening, and yet he chose to bring that bird-witted simpleton."

"I thought them admirably suited," Lydia said, still seething from Blackthorn's audacity.

"Not my cup of tea, but she is rather pretty," Cedric offered in defense of his former officer.

Both ladies looked at him as though he were suffering from fatigue, and he hastily asked if they would see Miss Osborne at Almack's the following night.

Lydia glanced at her friend in surprise. "Are you attending, Perdita?"

"I promised Miss Gilbert I would. Her cousin has procured vouchers for her, and though one would think the escort of a duke sufficient entrée, the dear girl is frightened that no one else will speak to her. You remember what it was like your first Season, Lydia, and how intimidating we found Almack's."

"Heavens, do not remind me. For all our bravado, we were like a pair of shivering peahens. It was horrible, but we had each other to bolster our courage. Well, Miss Gilbert is a very nice girl, so perhaps I shall look in. I am promised to Mrs. Parnel, but need not put in an appearance until late."

"Thank you," Perdita said, then added softly, "Oh, botheration. Do not look now, but Miss Martin is bearing down on us. Justin must have seen her and made good his escape. She has been pursuing him with all the tenacity of a hound, and shows about as much breeding."

Lydia laughed. "I believe you insult Papa's hounds. They are very well-bred, while she is merely vulgar. I do not know why you allow her to disturb you, but if you wish, take your leave and I shall detain her."

Perdita did not hesitate. Linking her arm in Cedric's, she strolled quickly away. Miss Martin, arm in arm with Claudia Richards, saw her and quickened her own pace, but Lydia stepped directly into her path.

Sir George, deep in conversation with Sophia Remfrey, saw the maneuver and wondered briefly why Lydia would make an effort to speak to someone she normally took pains to avoid. For a few seconds, he considered joining her, but then Miss Remfrey claimed his attention again. Sir George settled back with a smile. After all, Lydia was quite capable of handling someone of Miss Martin's ilk, and he had not finished telling Miss Remfrey about his altercation with his tailor.

* * *

Lydia came down for breakfast at an advanced hour on Thursday. After spending some time at Almack's the evening before, they had looked in at Mrs. Parnel's, and the informal gathering proving most congenial, remained until the small hours of the morning.

Sophia, sitting opposite, complimented her niece on her pretty gown, then remarked, "Kind of you to take Miss Gilbert in hand. I do hope she is appreciative of your efforts."

Lydia, perusing her copy of the *London Gazette*, glanced up in surprise. "I did very little."

Sophia sniffed. "On the contrary, you did a great deal, my dear, strolling around the ballroom twice with her. It has been seen by everyone who matters that she stands on intimate terms with you, which can only be to her credit."

Laying down the paper, she stared across the table at her aunt. "I thought you liked Miss Gilbert. She seems a very sweet girl and not at all presumptuous."

"As to that, I do find her charming and can understand that you should befriend her, but my dear, *must* you throw her at the duke's head?"

Lydia laughed. "Is that what concerns you, Aunt Sophy?"

"Indeed it does. Such an agreeable man. It would have been quite a splendid match, only now he is looking at his young cousin in a very different light. I should not be at all surprised if an announcement is not forthcoming before the month is out."

"Well, I hope you may be right. Miss Gilbert has been enamored of him since the start. I noticed it that evening at the theater."

Vexed, Sophia shook her head. "Have you no thought to your own future? 'Tis past time you wed, my dear. I had thought that perhaps Mr. Saunders, but of course he is now entirely ineligible—so careless of him to have lost his fortune—I expect he will try to entice Miss Piedmore, and he may well do for her, but not for you. Of course it did not matter, not with the Duke of Lansing paying you court, which no one could deny would be a far superior match, but now that you have done all in your power to fix his interest with Miss Gilbert ... well, that leaves only Sir George."

"Only?" Lydia asked, raising her brows.

Sophy blushed. "Gracious, how you take one up. You must know I think the world of Sir George—such elegance, such style—only ... there is his mother, and I would be doing you a disservice, darling, if I did not caution you that she will do all possible to prevent such a match."

"What have you heard?" Lydia demanded.

Blushing more furiously, Sophia toyed with her teacup, unable to meet her niece's eyes directly. "I am sure 'tis nothing ..."

"Aunt Sophy," Lydia warned.

"Oh, dear, I did not intend to mention anything—I am almost positive there can be no truth in such a rumor. You know how dreadfully gossip spreads in this town—" she glanced up, encountered Lydia's determined gaze, and quickly lowered her own eyes. "She means to stop Sir George from offering for you."

Mary came in bearing a fresh pot of tea, giving Lydia a few moments respite in which to compose herself. When the maid had left the room again, she looked at her aunt, seemingly calm. Only the delicate brows angling away from her eyes gave one an indication of her anger.

"Does she, indeed?"

"Oh, dear, I never should have said a word. Only that odious Mrs. Ormond cornered me last night when you were dancing with Sir George, and she was so condescending—"

"What," interrupted Lydia in an awful voice, "precisely did she say?"

"She said," Sophia began, then had to swallow hard as the words seemed to stick in her throat. After a sip of tea, she continued, "She said it was a pity you were wasting your time with Sir George, and of course, I asked her what she meant. Such an obnoxious woman—I really cannot abide her."

"Then, why bother to speak to her?" Lydia asked.

"Oh, my dear, I could not *cut* her! Only think how unpleasant it would be. Why, just the notion turns my stomach queasy."

"You are a great deal too kindhearted," Lydia declared, buttering a croissant despite the butterflies in her own stomach. "Mrs. Ormond is not worth the tip of your little finger, and if she never spoke to either of us again, I could not think it a very great loss."

"Perhaps not, dearest, but it would be dreadfully awkward when so many of our friends are acquainted with her not to be on terms."

"I suppose, but do pray tell what else she said to put you in such a flutter."

Sophia saw there was no avoiding it and took her courage in her hands, saying in a rush, "Lady Weymouth is returning to town. It seems someone wrote her that Sir George had distinguished you with such a marked degree of attention that people were actually speculating on whether or not he would offer for you."

"Surely that is not all?"

"Well, no . . . not entirely. The *on-dit* is that Lady Weymouth wrote to her friend, Cecilia Fullerton, that she did not consider you suitable for her son, and she would put a stop to such nonsense as soon as she arrived in town."

When Lydia said nothing, she hurriedly added, "I am sure it is all humbug. The very idea that an Osborne would not be acceptable is ludicrous. Why, our family can trace their roots back to the twelfth century, and you may be sure I told Mrs. Ormond so. Lydia? Dearest, I mislike the look in your eye. Promise me you will not do anything rash."

Chapter 6

Miss Osborne was seen at the opera, the theater, numerous balls, and private dinners during the days following the conversation with her aunt. She gave every appearance of having nothing more burdensome on her mind than what color gown would be most becoming, or whether or not a new straw bonnet flattered her fair complexion.

Sophia, however, was not deceived and watched her niece with nervous apprehension, particularly so when they chanced to encounter Lady Weymouth shortly after her arrival in town. Lydia's manner toward the older woman was so exquisitely polite, deferential without being subservient; so much the young lady of impeccable breeding, that one should have been reassured. Sophia's alarm only increased. She would have felt better had Lydia uttered some cutting rejoinder or behaved with the flippant unconcern that had earned her the reputation of setting the style, rather than following it. Lydia minding her manners filled her with grave unease.

Had she been privy to her niece's thoughts, Sophia would have ignobly fled town, but Lydia wisely kept her opinions and her plans to herself. She thought of several devastatingly sarcastic remarks to make to Mrs. Ormond, Mrs. Stoneleigh, and Lady Weymouth, but swallowed them, showing instead a smiling countenance, and demonstrating a sweetness of manner that rivaled Miss Gilbert's.

On Friday, knowing Sir George's habits, she persuaded Perdita to drive with her in the park, and they had not been there above twenty minutes when he appeared. As their carriages drew even, she directed her groom to pull up.

After greetings were exchanged, she gave him the benefit of her dazzling smile and wide-eyed gaze, saying sweetly, "I do hope you are well, sir, and have not been ailing."

"No indeed, Miss Osborne, but if I were, seeing you today would certainly act as a tonic. Most becoming hat, if I may say so, my dear."

"Why, thank you, Sir George," she replied, her long lashes sweeping down over her expressive eyes.

"And your dear aunt, is she well?"

"Quite, but I fear she thinks you have deserted us. We have not seen you in Cavendish Square for several days."

"I am flattered you noticed my absence," he replied, his chest swelling a little, "but I assure you it is not from want of desire, but due to a number of pressing engagements that I have not called. My mother, you know, arrived in town quite unexpectedly."

"Yes, delightful to see her again. We met her at Mrs. Drummond's on Friday, but though we are all pleased to welcome her return, I cannot regard it as a blessing if it means we shall see less of you, sir."

This was said so archly, and was so patently a lie, that Perdita nearly choked on a gurgle of laughter.

Had Lydia said as much to Justin, he would have instantly been on the alert. Sir George, however, possessed that persuasion of mind which enabled him to believe any amount of flattery, no matter how outrageous. Much encouraged, he replied boldly, "No one, not even my dear mother and the dutiful attendance that must naturally devolve on a son, could keep me long from your presence, Miss Osborne. Indeed, I was intending to call on you tomorrow."

"Oh, how unfortunate! I am promised to Lord Dryden," she said, naming the one gentleman with whom he indulged a friendly rivalry and was certain to incur his jealousy. "He has promised to let me try the paces of the new grays he purchased from Stanhope, though I am nearly certain I shall be home later . . . unless something comes of our scheme to visit Vauxhall. I did mention to him how much I should like to see the gardens again. Miss Piedmore was telling me they have made vast improvements, did you know? And tomorrow evening is the one time I have free."

"Then, you must let me escort you," George said, instantly rising to the bait. "I shall get up a party. Perhaps Miss Lambert and Mr. Richmond would care to join us?"

"What a charming notion," Perdita murmured.

"Consider it settled, then," George declared, smiling at Lydia. "I shall procure a box in one of the colonnades, and we will dine there, if that is agreeable?"

"Perfectly, sir."

"My regards, then, to your aunt." His horses were growing restive, several carriages were waiting to pass, and courtesy demanded he take his leave. He did so reluctantly, caught once more in the spell of Lydia's beauty.

When they were out of earshot, and mindful of the groom, Perdita whispered, "What mischief are you brewing?"

"Why, my dear, I do not know what you mean."

"Balderdash. Do not play the innocent with me. Sir George may be caper-witted enough to believe you have a sudden yen to visit Vauxhall, but you are not pulling the wool over my eyes. What do you intend by it?"

"Come and see for yourself."

Perdita had to be content with that, for Lydia could not be brought to say another word about her plans, and spent the remainder of the drive enlargening her plans for the party to include the Duke of Lansing, the Gilbert ladies, her aunt Sophy and Mr. Fortescue, Miss Piedmore and Mr. Neville.

Perdita shook her head. "I can understand, perhaps,

74

inviting Miss Gilbert, for she is very nice, but must you include her mother? And why Miss Piedmore and Mr. Neville?"

Lydia, with a cat-in-the-cream smile, replied airily, "Oh, they know everyone and talk excessively. If anything vastly exciting should occur, we can be sure the news would rapidly spread among the *ton*."

"I have the most dreadful feeling that I would be wise to remain quietly at home."

"But I particularly want your company," Lydia purred. "Promise me you will come. Which reminds me, how is your brother?"

"Well enough," Perdita replied guardedly.

"Splendid." The carriage rolled to a stop in front of the Lamberts' residence, and as Perdita prepared to step down, Lydia added, "Do give dear Justin a message for me. Tell him we are all going to Vauxhall, and that he would do well to, I believe the term is, *hedge his bets*."

Perdita, standing on the pavement, her brow furrowed and a worried look in her brown eyes, gazed up at her friend. "Lydia, you must tell me—"

"Sorry, darling, I really must hurry. I shall see you tomorrow."

On Saturday morning, Lydia awoke in a melancholy mood. Light was beginning to seep in the windows, and unable to return to sleep, she sat up in bed, considering her future. All her plans were in place, and nothing now remained except to execute them. She had little doubt she would succeed, for Sir George had been on the verge of proposing several times during the last two years. It would be relatively easy to maneuver him into making an offer this evening as they strolled in the romantic lamp-lit gardens . . . if she truly wished to do so.

Therein lay her dilemma. Justin's certainty that she would never be able to wed Sir George had spurred her determination to prove she could, and it had been further fueled by Lady Weymouth's declaration that she considered Miss Osborne an unsuitable bride for her precious son.

Lydia meant to prove them both wrong, not that her decision had anything to do with Justin. She told herself it was high time she married; certainly she had formed that intention before his return to town, and she had for several years considered Sir George as a possible husband. He was attractive, agreeable, considerate, thoughtful . . . only the notion of spending the rest of her life with him did not excite those tender feelings in her heart that she had once experienced herself, and seen again when Perdita announced her engagement.

She told herself she was being foolish; there were more important things in life than a silly passion that would almost certainly dim with the years. Sir George was everything desirable in a husband, and she was sincerely fond of him. Surely, given time and the proximity of marriage, she would come to regard him with a deep and abiding affection such as her parents shared.

Impatient with herself and the dark mood that threatened her plans, Lydia rang for Finch. She waited for several moments, and after observing that the light edging the curtains was brilliant enough to indicate the morning well advanced, wondered that no one had yet brought up her morning chocolate. She was about to pull the bellpull again when her dresser stepped through the door.

"Beggin' your pardon for the delay, Miss Lydia, but there's been an upset in the house," Finch said, setting her tray down across Lydia's lap, then crossing to the windows to draw open the curtains.

"Indeed?" was the ominous reply. Lydia was not a stern mistress; she treated her servants kindly and generously, but in return, she expected her household to run smoothly.

"I did warn you how it would be," Finch said by way of apology.

"If this is about Mary, I have told you the girl will not be long with us. Miss Piedmore has agreed to engage her, so please do not let me hear any further complaints about her."

"I doubt you will, not now," the tall dresser replied with something like a most impertinent chuckle.

Lydia glared at her over the brim of her cup. After taking a sip of the chocolate, she set it down, then sighed. "All right, Finch. Open your budget. It is plain something dreadful has occurred that obviously involves Mary."

"I believe you'll be changing your mind about her, Miss Lydia. Why, to think only yesterday you was telling me how she's a shy country girl and not up to snuff, but she was up to something right enough. I suspicioned it, but—"

"Finch, cut line."

"If you want the wood with no bark on it, she's done run off with Henry! After bamboozling us that she was such a proper one—well, shabbing off with the second footman in the middle of the night is not what I call proper behavior. And, after all you done for her, leaving only a note for Mrs. Barrows. Disgraceful behavior, I call it."

For a moment Lydia was stunned. She wondered why Mary hadn't come to her. She certainly would not have objected to the girl's marriage, and would have given the couple a handsome bride present.

"Mr. Applewood is rare upset, I can tell you," Finch continued, "but he knows, as do the rest of us, that it was that girl's doing. She—"

"Enough, Finch. You will please inform the staff that I fail to see why Mary's departure, however sudden, should throw the household into turmoil, and that I shall be down to breakfast shortly, and will expect to see some semblance of normalcy or will know the reason why. When you return, you may lay out my jonquil walking dress."

Finch, realizing it would be most unwise to provoke her mistress further this morning, nodded silently and backed from the room.

Order seemed to be restored when Lydia went down to breakfast, but she knew Mary's sudden departure would comprise the prime topic of conversation in the household for the next several days, or at least until some more shocking scandal occurred.

Even Aunt Sophy, looking very sweet in an apple green morning dress, and a mobcap with a green ribbon perched atop her chestnut curls, could barely wait until the footman had left the room before remarking, "Good morning, my dear. Did Finch tell you about Mary? I do not know what the world is coming to, but I will say this; she had no cause to leave in such a disagreeable manner."

Lydia kissed her aunt's brow, took the seat opposite, and picked up the *London Gazette*. "I suspect Mary was driven out of the house by the other servants. They were not entirely kind to her, you know."

"Except Henry," Sophy said, a faint blush coloring her cheeks. "Gracious, when I think of all the times he has waited on table or carried my packages, and I never had the least notion he was harboring a grand passion."

Lydia, much amused, looked across the table. "How should you, Aunt? 'Tis not as though one breaks out in spots."

"You no doubt think me foolish, but I do believe one cannot help showing some indication if one is truly in the throes of love."

"Not foolish, but I do think perhaps you have been reading too many novels from the penny press. In real life, people behave very differently than those in your books. That last one you gave me, *The Grievous Gentleman,* was so absurd as to be ridiculous."

Sophy, looking offended, protested, "I will own that Miss Enderberry swooned rather more than one would think reasonable, but when Mr. Fairadon rescued her from that evil Lord Shanks and they eloped to Gretna Greene, well I thought it was wonderfully touching."

"There! That is precisely the sort of nonsensical behavior I mean. Do you not recall last year when Miss

Westhaven eloped because her parents would not consent to her marriage? I do not recollect his name, but he was a younger son without prospects save for a living as a vicar. No one would receive her when she returned, and the last I heard, she was residing in some remote village, and I am afraid, far from happy."

"Oh, dear," Sophy said, as she lathered butter and preserves on a roll. "I do wish you had not reminded me. 'Twas very sad."

"Quite. I cannot imagine what possessed Miss Westhaven. We were not well acquainted, but I always thought her a very prettily behaved girl."

"But darling, I do not think manners have ought to do with it. She must have been so much in love that she was lost to all other considerations. Of course it was very wrong of her, but I can understand how she might have felt. Shall I ring for more tea?"

Lydia shook her head as she emptied the last of the tea from the china pot into her cup. With a smile she said, "You are most persuasive, Aunt. I pray you are not thinking of eloping yourself?"

Sophy's gay laugh rang out. "Good heavens, as if anyone would wish to run away with me, not, of course, that I would consider such a step. Do you know, my dear, I think it must take a very brave person to do so. I fear I would never have the courage. Indeed, I am surprised Mary did."

The conversation lapsed as Sophia perused her letters and Lydia read the paper, but there was little news to hold her attention and she wondered idly what it would be like to elope. One would have to trust a gentleman without reservation, and be willing to sacrifice a great deal for his sake.

Unbidden thoughts of Justin Lambert sprang to her mind. Would she, at seventeen, have eloped with him had her parents forbidden a match? She'd been besotted enough, certainly, and convinced that she could not survive a mere year's separation from him . . . she recalled the days when her first thought in the morning was of

Justin, and how eagerly she would wait for him to call. And on occasion, when he did not come soon enough, she'd ridden out to meet him.

Justin had set her feet to dancing and awakened all the music in her soul so that she'd thought she'd burst from sheer happiness if she did not explode in song . . . she had been young and foolish, and perhaps if Justin had asked it of her, she would have agreed to an elopement.

"Lydia?"

She glanced up to see her aunt gazing at her oddly. "I beg your pardon, did you say something?"

"No, only . . . you looked so strange just then. What were you thinking of?"

"Oh, nothing really, just woolgathering."

"You cannot fool me, my dear," Sophy teased as she rose and gathered up her letters. "When a young lady looks as you did, it can only mean she is thinking of a certain gentleman. Not that I blame you, for he is sufficiently handsome and charming enough to occupy the mind of any lady."

Lydia stared at her aunt in considerable confusion.

Unaware of her misconception, Sophia continued, "What time is Sir George calling for us? I do hope it does not rain. Vauxhall is so pleasant when the weather is agreeable, but I loathe crossing in those small boats when a storm threatens, which I know you will say is silly of me, for they would not allow it were there any danger, but all the same it quite makes my stomach queasy."

"I believe he said seven," Lydia replied unsteadily. "Pray excuse me, Aunt Sophy. I must speak to Mrs. Barrows about finding a replacement for Mary."

Having made certain that Applewood understood Sir George would be calling at seven and was to be shown immediately into the drawing room, Lydia reposed on the gilded settee beside her aunt. She knew she looked her best. Her gown, fashionably low-cut, was of the fin-

80

est blue silk, embroidered with tiny seed pearls, and clung gracefully to her slender form. Her hair, shining from an application of egg yolks, followed by a rinse of rum and rose water, was softly pulled back from her face by a pair of ivory combs embellished with pearls, and fell in a shimmering cascade of curls to her shoulders. Even her feet were encased in delicate blue slippers that peeped out enticingly from beneath her gown.

The stage set, Lydia looked up expectantly as the door opened, and received her first intimation that the evening would not progress as she had expected.

"Lady Weymouth and Sir George Weymouth," Applewood announced before backing out of the room.

Sophy recovered first and rose hastily to her feet. "Why, Lady Weymouth, what a delightful surprise, and how charming you look."

"Save your flummery for those who believe it," the elderly doyen advised, then turned her piercing gaze on Lydia. "You will like as not catch cold in that skimpy gown, Miss Osborne. I suggest you wrap up warmly— the night promises a chill."

It did, indeed, Lydia thought, but she managed to smile sweetly as she replied, "How very kind of you to be concerned, but I am not yet of an age where one feels the cold. You will see that I am quite impervious to it, and truth be told, I find a hint of frost in the air rather invigorating."

"Hmmph," snorted Lady Weymouth, pulling the fur-trimmed heavy pelisse she had chosen to wear closer about her shoulders. A tall woman, she had never been deemed attractive, but people spoke of her as having a commanding presence.

The challenge lay between them, but before Lady Weymouth could respond further, Lydia turned to Sir George, playfully rapping him on the arm with her fan. "Fie on you, sir, for not informing us we were to have the pleasure of your mother's company."

"I did not know until this afternoon," he explained, tugging uncomfortably at his cravat.

"Stop fidgeting, George," Lady Weymouth ordered, laying a heavy hand on his arm. "Well, what are we waiting for? Do you mean to keep us standing here all evening?"

"Not at all, Mama," he muttered, and with an apologetic glance to the other ladies, led his mother from the room.

Fortunately, since Lydia defiantly refused to carry a shawl, the weather cooperated beautifully, producing a splendidly warm evening—the sort of evening that encouraged young couples to stroll along dimly lit paths, the sort of evening made for romance. Under other circumstances, Lydia would have been vastly pleased, but there was nothing the least romantic about sitting opposite Sir George in a closed carriage, with his mother's disapproving eye upon her. Wisely Lydia did not complain. She sat quietly, letting Aunt Sophy carry the conversation, and merely biding her time until she could succeed in speaking to George alone.

However, his mother proved to be a formidable opponent, and seemed determined to block Lydia at every point. It was Lady Weymouth who had the ordering of the carriages, and Lady Weymouth who directed the party's crossing in the small boats. Naturally she went first, and demanded the company of her son to steady her. Although she carried a cane, and leaned heavily on it, Lydia had long suspected that Lady Weymouth used her supposed infirmity as a means of controlling her son—a ploy that worked admirably.

The water was as still as glass, and the crossing to Vauxhall accomplished so smoothly and easily that even Sophy declared it to be entirely charming. Normally Lydia would have agreed, and been delighted by the enchanting vista spread before them. But she was annoyed with George for bringing his mother along, and her ire only increased when she learned Lady Weymouth had arranged the seating to her satisfaction.

The gardens were comprised of eleven acres, but the principal part was the grove: a large, shady area enclosed by four colonnades, midway along which was the vast shell that housed the orchestra. Each of the long colonnades contained a number of private boxes, horseshoe-shaped with the opening looking out on the grove. Unfortunately these were small, seating no more than six, and Lady Weymouth accordingly divided the party into two groups that would occupy adjacent boxes.

On the pretext of needing her son's assistance, Lady Weymouth kept George beside her, then quickly asked Miss Lambert and Cedric Richmond to join her, saying she wished to inquire about Miss Lambert's parents. She then claimed the company of the Duke of Lansing as an old friend, and reluctantly indicated Sophia Remfrey should also join her little party.

With a sweetness belied by the gleam in her eye, Lady Weymouth declared that since Lydia had invited the others as her particular guests, she would no doubt wish to sit with them during dinner. Accordingly, a short while later, Lydia found herself seated between Miss Nancy Gilbert and Mr. Felix Neville. Mr. Fortescue sat on Miss Gilbert's left, next to Mrs. Gilbert, and Miss Piedmore sat on Felix's right. The only way Lydia could even see Sir George was to lean around the partition that divided the stalls—conduct which, had she attempted it, would have immediately been declared extremely unbecoming.

Lydia determined to make the best of the situation. The night was still young, and she would contrive by some means to gain Sir George's escort for a stroll through the gardens after dinner. Until then, she decided not to let Lady Weymouth know that she'd succeeded in irking her. Using all of her charm, Lydia drew Miss Gilbert into an amusing conversation about her impressions of town life, and teased Mr. Neville over a recent wager he'd lost concerning a pig.

Mr. Fortescue declared that considering the ridiculously high prices they were charged for the miserly thin slices of ham served at dinner, they would have done well to bring their own pig, and a lively, silly discussion ensued concerning how best to roast it in the grove.

Mrs. Gilbert, perhaps more at ease without the presence of titled gentlemen, recounted a highly embellished tale about a man she categorized as a "boar" and whose manners were much worse than many pigs she had known. She was later moved to remark to her daughter that Miss Osborne was not nearly so high in the instep as she had at first believed. The laughter from their box could clearly be heard in the adjacent one.

Sir George, who politely excused himself after dinner to attend to a call of nature, strolled by their box on his return and stopped. He spoke politely to his other guests, then took a seat beside Lydia as Mr. Fortescue begged leave to be excused for a few moments.

His voice low, Sir George said, "I do not need to inquire if you are enjoying yourself."

"No, indeed, sir. Seldom have I experienced a more delightful evening, and I must thank you for arranging it."

"The arrangements are not entirely what I should have liked," he confessed, "but I am content as long as it has provided you some little pleasure."

"You are most kind," Lydia replied, modestly lowering her lashes. "We are proposing a walk later to better hear the orchestra, if you would care to join us?"

"Now, that I should enjoy above all things," George declared, but broke off as a loud pounding sounded on the side of the box. Lady Weymouth had grown impatient, and was plying her cane to good purpose.

"I shall see what I can contrive," he promised before hurrying back to his own box.

Lydia watched him leave, then had the uncomfortable sensation that she was being observed. She glanced around and saw Lord Blackthorn standing amid a group of young people in the grove. It was easy to distinguish his tall, broad-shouldered figure from the others. He nodded in her direction, excused himself from his party, and strolled toward her box.

"Why, Miss Osborne," he greeted her, his blue eyes full of devilment. "What a pleasant surprise, though now I think on it, I believe Perdita mentioned you planned to visit the gardens. But I am nearly certain she said Sir George was to be your escort."

Lydia managed to reply coolly, "Our party is rather large. Sir George and your sister are in the adjacent box."

His brows rose in exaggerated surprise. "Really? Odd, I would have thought that such an ardent admirer would have insisted on being by your side."

Mrs. Gilbert pushed her way forward. Emboldened by several glasses of wine, she thrust out her hand. "Lord Blackthorn, is it not? I am Mrs. Gilbert, and honored, sir, to make your acquaintance."

Justin, because it was clearly expected of him, bowed over the older woman's hand and kissed the air above her glove. "Charmed, madam."

"I believe you know my daughter," Mrs. Gilbert tittered, and waved a languid hand toward the table.

Nancy, sitting beside Mr. Fortescue, smiled shyly in his direction.

"I believe we have met, but I would be pleased to renew the acquaintance," Justin said. "Perhaps I might be permitted to join your party later?"

"Oh, dear sir, we would be positively thrilled, would we not, Miss Osborne?"

"Thrilled," Lydia muttered with a withering look at Justin that belied her words. "But I am sure his lordship must have his own party, and we should not detain him."

"Not at all," he drawled. "I find myself unaccountably deserted by my friends."

"Obviously people of discriminating taste," Lydia murmured, but her words were drowned out by Mrs. Gilbert's gushing, enthusiastic insistence that Lord Blackthorn join them at once. Only Justin heard her,

85

and the merriment in his eyes told her he was clearly enjoying himself.

Lydia reached for her wineglass.

Chapter 7

"What a delightful young man," Mrs. Gilbert pronounced when Lord Blackthorn left them for a few moments. "I must say I had not looked to enjoy myself so thoroughly this evening, and to think I nearly refused to allow my Nan to come."

"Did you?" Lydia asked politely while trying to figure a means of arranging a walk in Sir George's company, preferably before Justin returned.

"Indeed, yes. I may be new to town, but I have heard tell of Vauxhall and how more than one young lady had been lured into behaving, shall we say, indiscreetly?" She took another sip of wine, leaned forward, and confided, "But of course when I heard you were of the party, and His Grace, well, I knew it would be unexceptional. And now to have Lord Blackthorn join us, well, I tell you frankly, Miss Osborne, that I never thought to see my little girl moving in the first circles."

Lydia smiled as she glanced across the table at Miss Gilbert, deep in conversation with Miss Piedmore and Felix Neville, and replied absently, "She is a charming girl."

"She would be pleased to hear you say so, for I must tell you, she quite admires you; if there is any situation in which she is not entirely sure what to do, why she asks herself what Miss Osborne would do, and then behaves accordingly. She has said to me a dozen times, Miss Osborne would not do this, or Miss Osborne would think this vulgar, until I am all out of patience with her."

Lydia, who found the notion of being a pattern card of behavior for anyone alarming, sought to change the subject, and immediately suggested a stroll through the grove.

"But, Miss Osborne," Mrs. Gilbert protested. "We cannot leave yet—we must wait for Lord Blackthorn. He promised to return in a few moments."

Lydia rose gracefully to her feet. "You may wait for him if you wish, but I would not be surprised if he forgets us entirely. He has so many other friends here, you know."

"Well, there you are wrong," the older woman said, and tittered as a hiccup escaped her lips. "Here he comes now."

Lydia whirled around. She saw Justin a little distance across the grove, striding determinedly toward them, and a very unladylike retort rose to her lips. Suppressing it, she managed a smile. "So he is. Do pray excuse me. I must let my aunt know of our plans."

In her haste to leave the box before Justin reached it, Lydia collided with Mr. Fortescue, returning from the opposite direction. The cup of wine he was carrying sloshed over the brim and splashed down the front of her gown.

"My dear Miss Osborne, I am so sorry. Dreadfully clumsy of me."

"Not at all, sir. It was entirely my own fault," Lydia replied, knowing it was the truth but vexed with Mr. Fortescue all the same. She brushed futilely at the rapidly spreading stains, wondering if it would not have been better to remain at home. Nothing seemed to be going as she had planned.

"Try this," Justin said from behind her, and offered his handkerchief.

She took the cloth wordlessly and dabbed at her gown, but silk spotted horribly, and the damage was done. At least it was growing dark, and she could hope that the stains would not be very noticeable.

"Spilled your wine, Miss Osborne?" Lady Weymouth

asked derisively as she entered the box, leaning on the Duke of Lansing's arm. "I personally limit myself to one glass during dinner."

Lydia glanced up at the circle of faces suddenly surrounding her while Mr. Fortescue attempted to explain how the mishap had occurred. On Lady Weymouth's other side, Sir George stood helplessly, plainly ill at ease. In the babble of voices that followed, Lydia caught Perdita's murmur of sympathy, Aunt Sophy's cry of dismay, and Miss Gilbert's offer to loan her a shawl. She appreciated their concern, but wished they would all go away. It was embarrassing, and for a moment she longed to disappear in the shadowed walks lining the grove. Then she heard Justin's deep-throated chuckle, and as she turned, saw the amusement in his blue eyes.

Her back stiffened, and she lifted her chin defiantly. "Thank you, but 'tis nothing," she said to Perdita, and waved away Miss Gilbert's shawl. "I believe my gown will dry very quickly if I just walk about a bit. Sir George, would you be so good as to give me your escort?"

"Why . . . why certainly," he said.

Lady Weymouth instantly objected, "Surely you do not expect me to traipse all over the grounds, or do you merely intend to abandon me here?"

"Oh no," Sophia Remfrey protested. "I am certain you would be much more comfortable sitting here, and I shall bear you company, for although it is very pretty, I dislike walking about in the dark."

"You'd do better to go with your niece, or do you make it a habit of allowing her to wander off unchaperoned?"

Mrs. Gilbert tittered. "Well, that she won't be, my lady, for my Nan was saying as how she'd like to walk a bit, and I'll go along with the pair of them."

It was quickly decided that all the younger people would stroll as far as the orchestra, watch the fireworks, and then return to the box. Lady Weymouth gave up the battle, and after admonishing George not to tarry over-long, for she was exceedingly tired, settled heavily in a chair.

Lydia led the way, propelling George along with her. She walked briskly, ignoring the display of lamps illuminating the boxes and theater, and the tiny lights that glittered along the dozens of pathways. Although it was not intentional, in a very few moments they were well ahead of the rest of their party, and soon became separated by the vast swell of people around the orchestra enclosure.

"My dear, I realize you are somewhat agitated, but must you rush off as though the hounds are after you?"

Lydia glanced at him in surprise. She had very nearly forgotten his presence, so intent was she on putting as much distance as possible between herself and Lady Weymouth. Slowing her steps, Lydia apologized sweetly, and then said, "I suppose it is unreasonable of me to be annoyed merely because I have not had an opportunity to exchange more than a dozen words with you this entire evening."

Sir George smiled and patted her hand. "Unreasonable it may be, but I find the notion highly flattering. I had not expected you to even notice my absence, surrounded as you were by so many of our friends."

Her lashes swept down, hiding the satisfaction in her eyes, but she replied on a teasing note, "Why, how can you say so, sir, when you must know how highly I value your company?"

"Do you, my dear? I confess, there have been times when I hoped that you might be willing to regard me as more than a friend, but I feared my own desire clouded my judgment."

He is sweet, Lydia thought, touched by the deep sincerity in his voice. She knew of no one more kind or thoughtful, and when they married, they would deal extremely well together. She would see that he never regretted offering for her. But, of course, she had to bring that about before anything else could be accomplished.

As they approached one of the many paths that crisscrossed the gardens, she remarked, "Heavens, the music is so loud, I can barely hear you speak. Perhaps if we were to walk a little way down this path, we could converse more easily."

George readily agreed. The night was warm, strains of Beethoven drifted on the air, and he had a beautiful woman beside him. He looked down at her pure, elegant profile, admiring the high cheekbones, the curve of her chin, and the way her hair turned to silver in the moonlight. He knew that if he succeeded in winning her hand, he would be the envy of every man in England.

He cleared his throat, and murmured, "Did I mention how becoming your gown is, my dear? That particular shade of blue reminds me of a goddess stepped down from the heavens."

"Even splashed with wine?" she asked, a trifle amused at the extravagance of his compliment.

"In my eyes, you look enchanting whatever you wear."

"Thank you. I know I may always depend on you to elevate my spirits," she replied as they rounded a curve in the path. Seeing a bench conveniently situated just ahead, Lydia suddenly stumbled. "Oh, I do believe I caught a pebble in my slipper. If I could sit down for just a moment?"

"Of course, my dear, let me help you," George responded instantly, and solicitously seated her. He knelt down before her on one knee, his hand outstretched. "Would you allow me the privilege?"

Lydia lifted her skirt a modest inch or two and proffered her delicately shod foot. She felt George's gloved hands on her ankle, and was about to tease him when a movement beyond caught her attention and she glanced up.

Her scream shattered the night.

The man, tall, heavyset, and clad totally in black, appeared suddenly out of the darkness of the woods. He attacked swiftly. George, already off balance as he knelt on one knee, sprawled on the pathway. But as he tumbled forward, he grabbed his assailant's boot and pulled him down. Lydia watched, horrified, as the pair wrestled before her.

Her cries for help apparently unheeded, she glanced around for some sort of weapon and found a heavy branch lying behind the bench. Grabbing it up, she wielded it like a club above her head, waiting for her chance. It was hard to see in the dim light, but she saw the flash of George's stock as he was thrown on his back. Using all of her strength, Lydia swung the branch down on the footpad's shoulder.

Unfortunately, George shifted just as she struck, and he took the full weight of the blow. As he collapsed, his grasp on the other man weakened and his assailant easily threw him off. The footpad grabbed Sir George's purse, rose unsteadily to his feet, and then insolently touched his hand to his cap, nodding at Lydia. "Thanks for the help, miss."

Incensed, Lydia watched helplessly as the thief disappeared into the woods as quickly as he had come, then she flew to Sir George's side. He wasn't moving. She knelt beside him, cradling his head in her lap. "Oh, say something, please. I am so sorry—I only meant to help, but—"

"What the devil is going on here," Lord Blackthorn demanded as he rounded the curve in the path. Perdita and Cedric Richmond followed just behind him.

"Justin! Oh, thank heavens you have come," Lydia cried. "We were set upon by a footpad. He came out of the woods over there," she explained, waving a hand in the general direction. "If you hurry, you may be able to catch him."

Justin stared at her, his eyes stormy. "What were you doing out here?"

"Does that matter now?" she demanded. "Sir George is hurt, and that thief stole his purse. Aren't you going to do anything?"

Perdita knelt beside her. "How bad is he hurt?"

George groaned and opened his eyes. Lydia's face floated above him. "He did not . . . harm you?"

"No," she whispered, tenderly brushing his hair off his brow. "Lie still until a doctor can tend to you."

"No need," George rasped and struggled to sit up, but he couldn't help wincing as his shoulder throbbed with pain.

"Lord of mercy, what has happened?" Mrs. Gilbert demanded, coming up on the scene with Mr. Fortescue. Felix Neville escorting Miss Piedmore, and the duke with Miss Gilbert, followed on her heels.

"A footpad set upon Sir George," Cedric informed her tersely. "I've heard reports that a band of them are operating in the woods here. 'Tis getting so it's dangerous to stray from the lighted walks."

"Is he hurt?" Miss Piedmore asked, staring in fascinated alarm.

Justin and Cedric between them got Sir George to his feet. He was groggy, and leaned heavily against them, but remained insistent that he did not need a doctor.

Perdita placed a comforting arm around Lydia's shoulders as they stood watching. "How perfectly dreadful for you, Liddy. Justin said he thought he heard someone scream—was that you?"

She nodded. "He came out of nowhere. I had a . . . a pebble in my slipper and had stopped to remove it . . ."

"A pebble?" Justin questioned, his voice rife with mockery. "How very original."

Lydia whirled on him. "Surely at some time or other, you must have known someone to get a pebble lodged in their shoe."

"Oh, any number of people, not to mention dozens of young ladies who have suddenly sprained an ankle, or had their carriage break down in front of my gate—"

"If you are implying that I deliberately—"

"Children, children," Mrs. Gilbert interrupted. "This is no time to be squabbling. We must think what is best to do."

"I rather thought *someone* would go after the thief," Lydia snapped, glaring at Justin.

"If you think I am going to go chasing after a footpad in complete darkness over eleven acres of woods, you have obviously lost what little sense I once thought you possessed."

"And you, Lord Blackthorn, are not nearly as brave as you pretend!"

Cedric hastily intervened. "It would be foolish, Miss Osborne. These footpads know the woods. Without an organized search party, we wouldn't stand a chance of finding the man."

"You must consider Sir George," Perdita murmured. "We should get him back to the box."

"Yes, but not in that condition," Mrs. Gilbert declared. "Why, only think what Lady Weymouth would say. And you, Miss Osborne, there is dirt all over your gown. If the pair of you return to the box looking like that, why gossip would spread over London faster than the great fire ever did."

"She is right," Perdita agreed, "but I do not see what else we can do."

Mrs. Gilbert took charge and turned to Mr. Fortescue. "Do you have one of those flasks you gentlemen always seem to carry?" When he nodded sheepishly, she directed him to give Sir George a drink, then turned to Mr. Richmond. "You are of a height, and your coat is the same color as his. If you'd be willing to exchange coats, I think we may contrive to brush through this tolerably well."

Cedric grinned as he shrugged out of his coat. "I am willing, madam, but what am I to do? Surely someone will notice I am missing my coat."

"You, sir, will escort Miss Lambert and Miss Osborne home. I believe if you leave now, and skirt the crowds, no one may notice your lack of a coat or the state of her gown. Nan! Nan, give her your shawl—it will help to cover the worst of the damage."

"And what part am I to play in this masquerade?" Justin demanded.

Mrs. Gilbert smiled at him. "You, my lord, may escort Miss Remfrey home. I am sure she will be concerned over Miss Osborne, and you will no doubt know best how to soothe her. Tell her that her niece was suddenly taken ill, and Miss Lambert has taken her home."

"Very well, madam, but I fail to see what you think all this will accomplish."

"I hope, my lord, to avoid a lot of unnecessary gossip. I am very certain everyone here can be depended upon not to speak of this. Otherwise, Miss Osborne will be subjected to some very nasty innuendos. People will want to know what she was doing on this deserted path with Sir George—"

"Which is something I should like to know myself."

She fixed Blackthorn with a baleful stare. "That's betwixt you and her, my lord, but I won't stand by and see someone who has been as kind to my Nan as Miss Osborne, and as fine a lady as I've ever met, made the brunt of nasty jokes—not if I can help it. I've had my experience with such, and it's not very pleasant, I can tell you. Now, my lord, are you with us?"

Lord Blackthorn bowed gallantly. "At your service, Mrs. Gilbert."

Satisfied, she turned her attention back to Sir George, who had exchanged coats with Cedric Richmond. He still looked drawn and shaken, but unless one observed him closely, one would not think he'd been in a brawl. Giving him a nod of approval, she asked, "Can you walk unassisted, Sir George?"

"As long as I don't have to use my arm—egad, but it feels like he hit me with a club."

Lydia turned pale, but stepped forward and laid a gentle hand on his arm. "Sir George, I—"

"Do not say a word, my dear. I am entirely to blame for what has occurred, and I want everyone here to know that my . . . my intentions were completely honorable. If you permit me, I shall call on you tomorrow."

95

The sound of fireworks startled the group. Perdita urged Lydia, "Let us leave now, while everyone is distracted."

Too tired to argue, Lydia mutely agreed. But as she left the path, Justin blocked her way, an unfathomable look in his eyes.

"I want a word in private with you."

Perdita shook her head at her brother. "Not now, Justin. Can you not see that she is exhausted?"

He reluctantly stepped aside, but as Lydia started by him, he warned, "We will discuss this further when I bring your aunt home."

Chapter 8

Sophia Remfrey was prepared to admit Lord Blackthorn to the ranks of her friends, since he was dear Miss Lambert's brother. Nevertheless, there was an air of reserve about the gentleman that was missing in his sister and that made him seem rather unapproachable. Sophy stole a glance at him. Although he had treated her with consideration and thoughtfulness at Vauxhall, he had since lapsed into a brooding silence.

He lounged on the opposite seat of the carriage, staring out the window. His dark hair fell in disordered waves across his brow, as though he had run his fingers through it several times, and one hand drummed restlessly against his knee.

Sophy nervously cleared her throat. "Lord Blackthorn?"

When he looked around at her, she gathered her courage and asked, "Are you quite certain Lydia is not seriously ill or hurt?"

He gave a bark of laughter. "I can assure you, Miss Remfrey, that your niece is not hurt in any way—save perhaps for her pride."

Sophy shook her head. "If that is true, then I really do not understand why she had to leave with Miss Lambert. I fear you are keeping something from me."

"Not at all, ma'am, but perhaps it would be best to allow Miss Osborne to answer your questions. I believe we have arrived." Even as he spoke, the carriage came to a halt in Bedford Square.

Sophia, anxious to see for herself that Lydia was not

hurt, allowed Lord Blackthorn to assist her from the carriage, then thanked him. "It was kind of you to see me home, sir. I shall not detain you any longer."

"I will see you in, Miss Remfrey."

"That is not at all necessary, my lord. I perceive Applewood already has the door open."

"Then, I suggest we do not keep him waiting," he replied with a grim smile.

Sophy meekly acquiesced, wondering what all the young ladies saw in this gentleman to set their hearts aflutter. Of course he was handsome, and one could certainly not fault his figure, but there was nothing in the least congenial about his manners. She had the distinct impression that if she tried to deny him, he would not hesitate to make a scene.

She gave her gloves and shawl to Applewood and inquired about her niece.

"Miss Osborne is in the drawing room waiting for you, ma'am."

"Thank you," she murmured, and led the way down the hall. Lydia was sitting in one of the tall wing chairs near the fire, and Sophy crossed to her at once, holding out her hands. "My dear, are you ill? Lord Blackthorn assured me you were not, but I could not conceive what else would account for your leaving in such an odd way. I am sure I do not know what Lady Weymouth will say."

"No doubt a great deal," Lydia replied, but even as she rose and hugged her aunt, her attention remained fixed on Lord Blackthorn, who had followed her into the room. Glaring at him, Lydia demanded, "Come to gloat, my lord?"

Sophia shuddered at her niece's tone. "Lydia, dearest, you must still be overwrought. Lord Blackthorn was kind enough to drive me home, and insisted on coming in—I presume he wished to make certain you had arrived safely."

"Did you, my lord?" Lydia asked, an odd smile curving her lips. "If so, I am deeply gratified by your concern—however misplaced it may be—but as you may observe I am perfectly well, so allow me to bid you good evening."

"Always the charming hostess, I see, but tell me, Miss Osborne, who filled the role of knight-errant before I came to town? Rescue from your more impetuous suitors appears to be required on a rather frequent basis," he replied, his eyes insolently raking her figure. She had changed the blue gown for a simply cut jonquil dress, and brushed her hair so that it fell in soft waves to her shoulders. Nothing about her indicated that she had spent a distressful evening, but Justin suspected she was not nearly as calm as she appeared.

Deliberately provoking her, he taunted, "First there was Saunders a few weeks ago. If you will recall, I drove you home that night. Then, this evening—"

"This was entirely different," Lydia snapped.

Sophy looked in confusion from Blackthorn to her niece. "My dear, I do not understand—"

Ignoring her, Justin continued, "In what way? Twice now I have found you in some secluded locale with a gentleman intent on making improper advances."

Sophy sank into a nearby chair, fanning her flushed cheeks. "Improper advances . . . surely not . . . not Sir George?"

Lydia stamped her foot. "He was about to *propose*, my lord, and had he not been set upon by a footpad, he would have done so, and I would have accepted!"

Justin frowned in a parody of concern. "I suppose it is possible that was his intention, though when I offered for you, I distinctly recall seeking your father's permission first. Of course that was some years ago, and the rules governing polite behavior may have changed but—I beg your pardon, Miss Remfrey, did you say something?"

Sophy goggled at him. "I must not have heard you correctly, Lord Blackthorn. I thought you said that you . . . you once proposed to my niece?"

Justin nodded, watching Lydia, who'd obstinately

99

turned her back to him. "I did, and she accepted, but later jilted me."

Lydia whirled around. "I jilted you? How dare you say that? The choice was entirely yours, my lord, and need I remind you that you did not even hesitate."

Justin sauntered toward the sideboard and picked up the decanter. He glanced at Sophia, inquiring politely, "Do you mind?"

Stunned, she shook her head.

He poured a glass of brandy, then carried it with him to the fireplace. Leaning negligently against the mantel, he smiled at Lydia. "Is that how you remember it? I recall telling you that as soon as I returned from duty, we would be wed. It was you, my dear girl, who refused to wait for me. You would not even answer my letters, and when I came home on leave, you made it a point to be elsewhere."

Resentment flared in her eyes as all the old hurts resurfaced. Furiously she retorted, "You conveniently forget one minor point, my lord. I pleaded with you to resign your commission and marry me at once. But, of course, I meant so little to you that you would not even consider it. No, you just rode blithely off and expected me to sit home and knit you socks while I waited to hear if you had been wounded or killed."

His brows rose in an incredulous arc. "Not knit, Liddy—surely I never suggested knitting, though if you had known how, it would have made a touching picture."

Words failed her. She pivoted on her heel, heading determinedly to the door. After flinging it open, she turned around and glared at him. "I believe we have nothing further to say to one another, my lord. My aunt may be inclined to entertain you, but I am retiring. And do not call me Liddy!"

Justin winced as the door slammed shut behind her.

Sophy rose to her feet. She had occasionally witnessed her niece in an angry tirade, but never in such a fury as Lord Blackthorn seemed to engender in her. She suggested quietly, "Perhaps it would be best if you left now, my lord. I will have Applewood show you to the door."

He said nothing, but merely stood motionless, staring into his glass. Moments earlier he'd seemed full of devilment, treating Lydia with a sardonic humor, but when he looked up at Sophia at that instant, she saw only an agonizing pain in his eyes.

"Do you believe she intends to marry him?"

The question was wrenched from his heart. Sophy almost felt sorry for the man, and gestured helplessly. "I cannot answer you, my lord. Obviously I do not know my niece as well as I once thought."

"Nor I," he muttered, setting down the glass. "My apologies, Miss Remfrey. I will let myself out."

Despite his promise, Sir George did not call the following day, but sent a note around instead with his apologies. His mother, regretfully, had taken ill. Sophy called on her a few days later and reported to Lydia that Lady Weymouth seemed to have no notion that anything amiss had occurred at Vauxhall Gardens.

Lydia listened as she poured a cup of tea late that afternoon. It had been an exhausting day with numerous fittings for new gowns and the purchase of several bonnets. She had encountered any number of acquaintances, but so far there had not been the slightest hint of any rumors afoot. Miraculous, when one considered the number of persons who'd been present. Lydia handed her aunt a cup and inquired, "How is Lady Weymouth feeling?"

"She said her bones are aching dreadfully, and she finds it difficult to walk, but do you know, I think she may only want a little attention. My father was much the same way. I believe it is often so with elderly people who find themselves alone. 'Tis very sad."

Lydia smiled at her aunt. "You are a good deal too kindhearted, and see only the best in everyone."

"Perhaps, my dear, but if you intend to marry Sir

George, I think you must make an effort to win his mother over. She really is not so irascible once you come to know her—indeed, I found her most interesting. She was telling me of her childhood in Newmarket. Fascinating, really."

Lydia shook her head. "I shall leave you to establish peace between the families. May we expect to see Sir George soon?"

"Oh, heavens yes, I nearly forgot. He charged me to convey his warmest regards and to tell you that his sister, Lady Phipps, arrived this afternoon. She will sit with Lady Weymouth tomorrow, so he will be quite free to escort us to the balloon ascension."

"I shall look forward to it," Lydia said, but she sounded as though she were speaking of a trip to the tooth-drawer rather than a pleasant outing.

The lack of enthusiasm in her voice and a touch of melancholy about her eyes concerned Sophy. She reached across and touched her niece's hand. "My dear, you have not been yourself these past few days. If there is anything I can do—"

"Thank you, but I am just a bit blue-deviled," Lydia interrupted, and quickly changed the subject. But though she could avoid confiding in her aunt, it was far more difficult to escape her own thoughts. She remained tormented by the knowledge that Justin still held the power to disturb her.

If only he had not come back to town, Lydia thought. She had firmly set him from her mind, knowing how vastly unsuited they were. Justin was demanding, autocratic, arrogant, and impossible for someone of her temperament to live with. He required someone of Miss Gilbert's gentle mettle, who would greet his every utterance with appreciative awe and hasten to fulfill his every whim.

And she—she needed someone like Sir George, who would treat her with respect and consideration. She could be content with him, if Justin would only disappear again instead of continuously meddling in her affairs. Why he bothered, she could not imagine. He found fault with everything she said and did. Nor did it help that she heard of him constantly. If mere acquaintances were not singing his praises, Perdita was worrying over him.

On Tuesday, her friend had confided that Justin had not returned home from Vauxhall until noon the following day, and then could barely be brought to speak a civil word to anyone. Rumor had it that he'd partied all night with several of the Prince Regent's cronies.

"If that is true," Lydia said, "then he has no business censuring my conduct, for there is not a more rackety crowd in London."

"But you know it is not like him, Lydia. Justin never cared for drinking and gambling like some of those gentlemen. Cedric said he has never seen him like this. You may think it foolish of me, but I own I am deeply worried."

Lydia bit back a quick retort, for it was clear her friend was gravely troubled. Hugging Perdita, she said, "I do think it foolish. Come now, do you know any gentleman more capable of taking care of himself than Justin?"

Perdita had smiled weakly, but remained unconvinced. Remembering, Lydia frowned, then dismissed her thoughts. Justin never gave a tinker's rap about anyone or anything, and she'd be foolish to waste time worrying over him.

Accordingly Miss Osborne was seen that evening at Lady Sefton's, and later at Mrs. Parnel's, obviously in the best of spirits, and with nothing more pressing on her mind than deciding to whom she would grant the next dance. And if her eyes flew to the door at the entrance of each new arrival, well, no one had reason to suspect she was on the watch for anyone other than Sir George, who promised he would look in if his mother's uncertain health permitted his absence.

Lydia did not see him, however, until the following afternoon when he called at the house to escort them to

103

the balloon ascension in Green Park. Both ladies inquired after Lady Weymouth, who, it transpired, was resting in fair health.

George added with a warm smile for Sophy, "Mother asked me to express her gratitude for your visit the other day, and her hope that you will call again. If it would not be burdensome for you, I should appreciate it, for it seems to have improved her spirits no end."

"I would be delighted to do so," Sophy replied, hiding her own astonishment.

Lydia turned a gurgle of laughter into a fit of coughing, but managed to appear sweetly innocent when George glanced in her direction. His gratitude may have been for Sophy, but it was clear where his admiration lay. He complimented Lydia effusively on the stylish walking dress she had chosen. A rich deep blue, trimmed with black military-style braid, it suited her slender figure and, with the addition of a wide-brimmed hat, made her appear particularly feminine.

She thanked him sweetly, determined to do nothing today that would give anyone the least cause to find fault with her conduct or manners. During the carriage drive, she listened with commendable patience to a history of ballooning, though she wished George had spared them the tale of one unfortunate French gentleman. The poor wretch had, some years earlier, experimented with combining hot air and hydrogen, and been killed in an explosion. She could not quite rid her mind of the image the tale conjured up.

Sophy, too, expressed her horror, but George assured them, "I do not think we need anticipate anything so unpleasant today. Ballooning has made amazing progress—why, they are even parachuting from them now."

"How incredible," Lydia murmured.

"Indeed yes, my dear. Balloons may not quite be a common sight yet, but we have come a long way. Thirty years ago, when the first balloon landed outside Paris, it was set upon by a swarm of frightened peasants. They thought it was either an evil spirit or that a piece of the moon had broken loose and was coming down to crush them. They attacked it with dogs and pitchforks, and literally tore it to pieces."

"Oh, the poor dears," Sophy cried. "They must have been so terribly frightened."

"Undoubtedly, but they destroyed a great deal of work. Why, the bag alone took months to make, constructed as it was of a special varnished silk, and four days to fill with hydrogen. In order to protect future balloonists, the king had to issue a proclamation describing the balloons and telling his subjects not to be afraid of them."

As they reached the park and turned in, George pointed to his left. "If you will look over there, you may see where they are preparing the balloon for ascent." The ladies obligingly looked, but could see little other than a wooden enclosure where the wicker boat of the balloon was tethered. Several young men scurried about, intent on their business.

"We are most fortunate to arrive before they begin filling it, for that is a spectacular sight well worth witnessing," George explained as he found a pleasant spot in a shady grove where other carriages were already lining up. He carefully maneuvered his landaulet into position, and then asked his guests if they would enjoy a stroll, and perhaps a closer look at the balloonists.

The weather seemed perfect, one of those rare June days when it was brilliantly warm, and a little breezy, the sort of day that brought people to the park in droves. Lydia glanced around the grounds, already taking on the aspect of a festival. Carriages dotted the field, randomly hitched wherever a bit of shade offered respite from the sun, cloths were spread for impromptu meals, and throngs of people strolled about as though it were a fair. She waved to dozens of acquaintances, and remarked, "Gracious, most of London must be present."

"Can you wonder at it?" George asked. "Why, we are seeing history in the making."

Lydia agreed but found the preparations rather tedious. The large red-and-white silk that would form the balloon was still spread out on the ground and looked like little more than a tangle of material. She watched for some moments as two young men worked assembling the casks from which they would pipe the hydrogen into the balloon, then turned away to speak to Mrs. Parnel.

A few moments later, George called for her to come close to the enclosure and introduced her to Mr. Bellows, the younger of the two balloonists. He did not look to be above nineteen or twenty, had a freckled face and wide-spaced blue eyes, and an enthusiasm for flying that she found endearing.

"I could take you up one day, if you'd like to give it a try," he suggested after explaining how exhilarating it was to soar above the trees. "There is nothing in all the world to compare with it."

"Thank you, but no," she replied, laughing. "I shall take your word for it, for I have not your courage. Even looking down from a high-perch phaeton tends to frighten me."

"I would not allow anything to happen to you. You'd be as safe with me as in your own house, safer more like."

"No, sir. Thank you for the honor, but I shall watch you with both my feet on the ground. Good luck, Mr. Bellows."

Lydia started to turn away, but he called after her, leaning over the enclosure. "Miss Osborne?"

"Yes, Mr. Bellows?"

"I was wondering if maybe, well sometimes the balloonists carry a bit of luck with them—you know, like the knights used to do—a lady's scarf or handkerchief—"

She smiled gently at his red face and untied a deep blue ribbon from her curls, passing it across the enclosure to him. "I would be honored, Mr. Bellows. Please see you bring it down safely."

106

"Another conquest?" a deep voice murmured in her ear.

Lydia swung around. "Why, Lord Blackthorn, it seems one meets you everywhere."

"Only those who are exceptionally fortunate," he replied, undisturbed. "And where is your faithful lapdog?"

"I beg your pardon?" she said as she unfurled a pretty blue parasol and raised it over her shoulder.

Blackthorn laughed. "Well done, my dear, the very picture of innocence, but, of course, I was referring to Sir George."

"He is with my aunt, which you might have observed were not your eyes so bloodshot. Burning the candle at both ends, my lord?"

"How unkind of you to notice, especially when you look so enchanting that I am bereft of retaliation."

They had strolled a short distance away, and she glanced up at him curiously. "If true, my lord, it is assuredly a first."

He smiled down at her. "Have I been such a beast? No, do not answer. Instead, I propose a truce. It is far too lovely a day to quarrel. Shall we cry friends?"

"To what purpose, my lord?"

"If for no other reason, I hope to convince you to cease calling me 'my lord' in that odious manner."

Lydia hid a smile, pretending an inordinate interest in the preparations of the balloonists.

Justin flicked her cheek with his gloved finger to regain her attention. "We used not to treat each other so badly, Liddy. I find I miss those days."

"Don't," she cried, turning away from the touch of his hand. She didn't want him to be kind or gentle. She found it much easier to deal with him when he behaved like the arrogant aristocrat she knew him to be.

An odd look in his eyes, Justin dropped his hand and said quietly, "As you will my dear, but I hope we may at least observe the civilities for Perdita's sake. It distresses her to know we cannot meet without coming to points."

Was this some new ploy, Lydia wondered, hearing the deep sadness of his voice. One might almost think she had hurt him—deeply hurt him. It wasn't fair, and she was about to protest when a shout went up from the enclosure.

George came up at once with Sophy on his arm. "There you are, Miss Osborne. Afternoon, Blackthorn. My dear, they are starting to fill the balloon—it won't be long now before they launch it. Should you care to observe it from here, or would you be more comfortable in the carriage? I belive we may expect to see more of the actual process if we remain close at hand, but I have no doubt a splendid view of the balloon as it clears the trees might be obtained from some distance."

Lydia looked at the cagerness on his face, noted the way his eyes strayed toward the enclosure, and at once declared it would be much better sport to see the launch from the ground.

She had her reward when George bestowed a dazzling smile on her, and declared, "I knew you would think so. I took the liberty of reserving a space near the gate. Young Mr. Bellows is watching it for us, but I suspect we'd best hurry." Filled with good humor and bonhomie, he turned to Blackthorn and added, "You are welcome to join us, old man, if you wish. I doubt you'll find a decent place otherwise."

"Kind of you, Sir George. I meant to meet up with my sister, but I can't seem to find her in this crowd."

"Shouldn't try if I was you—you'll miss the launch." He led the way toward the gate, anxious now to make sure his space wasn't usurped.

It was like Sir George to be generous enough to include Justin in their party, but Lydia wished he had not done so. She found it difficult to keep her mind on the balloon, despite the air of expectation and excitement around them. Desperately she tried to concentrate on the tangle of silk as it slowly began to take shape. Gasps of surprise and admiration rose from the crowd as the bright colors merged into wide vertical stripes, and the immense size of the balloon hovered above them.

"I believe that young man is trying to attract your attention," Justin whispered some moments later.

She glanced up to see Mr. Bellows waving a blue ribbon at her from within the wicker basket. Apparently they were nearly ready to cast off the lines now. She gave the boy a small salute of encouragement, and called good luck. To Justin, she muttered tensely, "Oh, I hope he makes it safely!"

"I shouldn't worry," he advised. "These fellows pretty much know what they're about. They've got it down to a science now. As I understand it, it is merely a matter of controlling the valve at the top of the balloon. Unless there is—damn!"

Cries of alarm filled the grounds as the balloon suddenly veered sharply, placing it directly in the path of a towering tree.

"What is it? What's happening?" Lydia cried.

"The wind picked up—they're going to crash."

Chapter 9

Horrified, Lydia watched the balloon sail inescapably toward its doom. One moment it hovered some thirty feet above the crowd, the next it veered sharply, hurtling into the trees. The impact jarred the wicker boat. Young Bellows, leaning precariously over the side in a heroic effort to prevent the crash, was thrown from the basket. Screams rent the air.

Lydia strained to see as his body tumbled through the branches, caught once, then slipped again. He dropped like a boulder, bouncing off limbs until he was finally thrown to the ground. Even from a distance, she could see the bright red stain on his shirt.

Justin wasted no time. Shouldering his way through the mass of spectators, he made his way to the grove where the young balloonist had fallen—and Lydia followed on his heels.

She swallowed convulsively as she saw the boy sprawled on the ground, his face deathly white. Fearfully she noted the badly ripped shirt and breeches, the blood gushing from a brutal-looking gash on his arm, and the incredible stillness of his body. She watched Justin kneel beside him, his hands gently searching for injuries. "Is he . . . will he be . . ."

Justin tore the stock from his throat and glanced up at Lydia. "Let me have your handkerchief."

She withdrew it from her reticule and knelt beside them.

"Fold it into a pad," Justin directed, and indicated how she should place it over the cut on Mr. Bellows's arm, applying a steady pressure. He tied his own stock over it, stopping the flow of blood for the moment.

She gently brushed the boy's hair from his brow, and at her touch, his eyes flickered open. His gaze met Lydia's, and a ghost of a smile tugged at his lips. "Usually . . . safe," he murmured, before going off again.

"Justin, do something," she cried. She caught young Bellows's hand up in hers, holding it tightly as though she could give him some of her own strength.

"He needs more help than I can provide," Blackthorn said, sitting back on his heels. "He may be suffering from a concussion, and his right leg is probably broken. That cut on his arm will need stitches, too. But it's not hopeless, Liddy. If we could get him to the hospital—"

Behind them, a cheer went up as a group of men helped the older aeronaut descend from the tree. Tall with white hair, and thin to the point of emaciation, he was apparently more fit and agile than he appeared. Except for some minor scratches, he seemed unharmed and far more concerned with the damage to his balloon than that done either to himself or to his apprentice.

After curtly thanking his rescuers, he strode toward the crowd surrounding Mr. Bellows, took one look, and shook his head. "Now, what's to be done? I told the boy not to lean out the way he did—these young men won't listen. Had some idea he could somehow stop us from hitting the tree. How badly is he hurt?"

Justin told him, adding, "He needs to be taken to the hospital at once."

"That's entirely up to you, sir, but I can't be responsible. As it is, his carelessness has done incalculable damage, and I shall be hard-pressed to get the balloon repaired in time for the next exhibition."

His coolness was not well received by the onlookers, and a mutter of disapproval sounded around him. The aeronaut spread his hands helplessly. "I feel sorry for the lad, but he brought it upon himself. If he had listened to me—"

Lydia cut him short. Contempt for the man lacing her words, she demanded, "Where is his family?"

"That's just it, miss. Harry Bellows is an orphan, no kith or kin in this world that I know of, and I doubt very much if he has as much as a shilling to his name. Lives hand to mouth, like so many young men."

"Lydia!" Sophy Remfrey cried as she spotted her niece. "Oh, do come away." She came up with Sir George and after one horrified glance at the stricken boy, looked ready to swoon. "You have . . . your gown is . . . oh, merciful heavens."

"Do not look, Aunt Sophy," Lydia advised matter-of-factly, knowing her aunt's tendency to faint at the sight of blood. "Sir George, could you please take my aunt back to the carriage?"

"Certainly, but surely you do not intend to remain here? I must insist you come away with us and leave this to those whose business it is to tend to such matters."

Lydia, however, was not listening. Harry Bellows had stirred again, and his fingers tightened over hers.

"My leg . . . I can't move—"

"Hush," she said softly. "Lie still for the moment. We shall get you patched up." She turned her eyes in mute appeal to Justin. He answered her unspoken plea with a curt nod.

"Lydia, I cannot leave you here—" George began protesting.

"I will watch after Miss Osborne," Justin interrupted. "At the moment I need her assistance. You, sir, can best help by escorting Miss Remfrey home. My carriage is not far from yours—would you look for my man and tell him to bring it here at once? And if you see my sister and Mr. Richmond, tell them I have need of them."

As Sophy moaned at the same instant, and leaned heavily against his arm, George reluctantly agreed. He did not like it, but neither Miss Osborne nor Lord Blackthorn seemed inclined to listen to him, and Miss Remfrey obviously needed his assistance. Her face had drained of color, and the glassy look in her eyes told him she would soon faint if he did not get her away. He told Lydia he would take her aunt back to the carriage, then return for her.

Lydia had already forgotten his presence. She concentrated on keeping Harry Bellows as comfortable as possible, uttering soothing words of encouragement whenever he opened his eyes, and assuring the boy that they would take care of him. He looked so very young, and so helpless lying there, her heart went out to him.

Cedric Richmond appeared with Perdita a few moments later, and it was he who cleared a path for Lord Blackthorn's landau, and helped Justin and his groom carry the unconscious lad to the carriage. Perdita stood with her arm around Lydia until the boy was securely settled.

Justin stuck his head out the window. "Are you coming, Liddy? Your presence seems to soothe the boy." To Cedric, he said, "I'll take him to St. George's Hospital at Hyde Park. Bring Perdita and meet us there as soon as you can."

Lydia, who on the rare occasions when she was ill had Dr. Knightsborough come to her house, looked askance at the conditions at St. George's Hospital. Here the indigent came for treatment, crowding into the halls and waiting rooms, and overflowing into the courtyard. She saw soldiers with their arms or legs amputated, a woman whose face and arms were horribly burned, sickly children in tattered rags, and a number of young girls huge with child.

The matron refused to allow her in the examining room, showing Lydia instead to a private office where she could wait for Lord Blackthorn and news of Harry Bellows. But even ensconced in the tiny cubicle, which was drab and dirty, Lydia was not insulated from the sound of agonizing cries that rang continuously in the halls and wards.

Unable to sit quietly, she restlessly paced the confines

of the small room. She'd been waiting nearly thirty minutes when the door opened. Perdita, after thanking the waiflike imp who'd shown her the way, stepped into the room. Her small upturned nose wrinkled distastefully at the odor. "Lord, what a wretched place. Have you any news?"

Lydia shook her head. "Justin promised to let me know as soon as the doctor finished examining Mr. Bellows—but it has been so long. 'Dita, I am so afraid . . . that poor boy was so pale when they carried him in, and in such pain."

"I know, but you must not lose hope. Cedric told me he has frequently seen worse injuries on the battlefield, and men who survived against insurmountable odds. And do not forget that Justin is with him. That may sound like the partiality of a sister, but Cedric said I should tell you that your balloonist could have no one better beside him."

Lydia nodded. "I may fault your brother for any number of things, but his willingness to help in an emergency is not one of them. He was the only gentleman who tried to do anything for that boy—excepting your Mr. Richmond, of course. The rest stood there and watched as though they feared to dirty their coats."

Perdita smiled. "No, he never hesitates. Remember when little Tommy Tugrow nearly drowned in the river?"

"I had almost forgotten," Lydia mused. They had picnicked that day down by the Medley, she and 'Dita, Justin, Philip Chandler, his little sister, Meg, and Roland Dawes, who had a crush on Perdita. The memories came flooding back. "Justin stripped off his coat and dived in before the rest of us had a notion of what was afoot."

"And he was so angry when he found out Tommy had nearly drowned trying to save a sack of kittens. I shall never forget the look on Justin's face."

It was not his face Lydia remembered, but the way he'd looked coming out of the river—his shirt and breeches sopping wet, and molded to the lithe lines of his body. Even now, just the memory had the power to bring a blush to her cheeks. Embarrassed, she turned away from Perdita, and complained, "I wish someone would tell us what is happening. I loathe waiting like this. One feels so helpless."

Perdita sighed and sat down on the faded settee. "I am sure it will not be much longer. Cedric went to see what he could find out, and he will come to us as soon as possible."

She spoke softly, unaware of the note of sublime faith and pride her words carried, but Lydia heard and glanced at her friend with a touch of envy. Perdita was more fortunate than she knew to be engaged to a gentleman she obviously cared so much about. But this was not the time to be thinking of such things.

Lydia strode toward the door. "You may sit here and wait if you wish. I intend to find out what is happening."

The door opened before she reached it, forcing her to step back as Justin and Cedric crowded into the small room. "I was just coming to look for you," she said, anxiously searching his face for some sign.

"Dare I hope your impatience is due to missing me?" he teased as he caught up her hands. "No, do not fly up in the boughs, Liddy. I know you are concerned, but your balloonist will be fine, my dear."

"Oh, thank heavens," she murmured, and in her relief, allowed Justin to keep possession of her hands. "What did the doctor say? How badly was Mr. Bellows injured?"

"Two of his ribs are cracked, his arm required a number of stitches, and his leg is, as we suspected, broken. But he's young, relatively healthy, and Dr. Forbes is of the opinion he will mend rapidly, although this will undoubtedly put an end to his career as an aeronaut."

"I cannot regret it, but what is to become of him? I

do hate to think of him staying here. Justin, it is such a dreadful place—"

He looked over her head, exchanging an amused glance with Cedric. "You owe me five pounds." To Lydia, he explained, "I wagered you would feel that way, and I promise you, as soon as the boy is able, he will be moved. Cedric has agreed to put him up until he's recovered, and then Bellows will come to me. I believe he may make a passable groom."

She did not thank him, but the look in her eyes as she gazed up at him was sufficient.

Behind them, Cedric coughed discreetly. "I think we had best escort our ladies home, sir."

Abruptly recalling where she was, and with whom, Lydia hastily withdrew her hands. "Dear heavens, yes. Aunt Sophy will be dreadfully worried, only—do you think I might see Mr. Bellows before we leave?"

Justin shook his head. "Dr. Forbes does not advise it at present. He's given the boy a sedative, and he should sleep for several hours, but your balloonist gave me this to return to you." He pulled a blue ribbon from his pocket and handed it to Lydia. "He said to tell you he brought it back safely."

She smiled as she accepted it, but the sight of that frivolous piece of silk brought all the emotions she'd suppressed all day to the surface. Suddenly overwhelmed, tears misted her eyes and she ducked her head.

Justin placed a finger beneath her chin and gently lifted. "Come now, my dear one. The boy's fine, and if you like, I promise to bring you to visit him in a few days."

"Thank you," she murmured, embarrassed.

Perdita, in an effort to break the tension that filled the small room, hugged Lydia and declared, "I hope you are not planning to leave me out of this expedition. I wish to visit the boy as well."

Cedric cuffed his former major on the arm. "Rank may have its privileges, but you cannot just invite young ladies to call at my house. Need I remind you that mine is a bachelor establishment?"

"We will devise something," Justin said, leading the way out of the room. "Unless, of course, you fear that Perdita will take your true measure and withdraw from the betrothal? I warn you, my dear sister, he is not the neat and orderly gentleman you think him. Why, if you had seen the way he lived in camp—"

"Unfair," Cedric protested. "I defy any gentleman, save yourself, to maintain immaculate living quarters under the conditions we endured on the Peninsula. And if it were not for that extraordinary batman you had, you, sir, would have been in the same dire straits as the rest of us."

The two gentlemen kept up a meaningless flow of nonsensical banter as they escorted Perdita and Lydia to the street, effectively distracting the ladies from the sights and sounds of the injured and maimed who still awaited treatment.

Once outside, while Perdita spoke quietly to Cedric a few feet away, Lydia tried to thank Justin for all he'd done, but he dismissed her words with a wave of his hand.

"In truth, I should not have brought you here."

A bit of her old spirit returning, she assured him, "If you had not, I would have followed with Perdita and Mr. Richmond."

He grinned. "I suspected as much, but it was not very prudent of either of us. I always disliked London because it was a hotbed of gossip, and it has not improved during my absence. I think you would have been wiser to have returned home with your aunt."

"As if I cared what a few old tabbies have to say."

"You may not, but I rather suspect Sir George does, and if you truly mean to wed him—"

"I do," she interrupted, a challenge in her voice.

For once Lord Blackthorn chose not to argue, but merely nodded somberly. "Then, I suggest you have a care for appearances. That carriage that just passed us

117

belongs to Mrs. Fullerton, who, if I am not much mistaken, is an intimate of Lady Weymouth's and one of the worst tattle-mongers in town."

Pretending a nonchalance she was far from feeling, Lydia shrugged, but for all her bravado, she did not protest when Justin insisted she drive home with Perdita and Mr. Richmond.

"You must not worry over her," Sophy told Sir George as they sat over a cup of tea in her drawing room. "Lydia has always been . . . well impulsive, I suppose one would say. She has an exceedingly kind heart that, unfortunately, sometimes leads her to act without weighing the consequences."

"But to go off in that manner—without a word to me, or, I might add, to you, shows a shocking want of conduct. Why, were it not for Mrs. Parnel seeing her leave in Lord Blackthorn's carriage, we would have no notion of what has become of her."

"I know," Sophy said sympathetically. "And I do not mean to make excuses for her, but she was so concerned over that boy's injuries, I fear it drove all other considerations from her mind. She never could bear to see anyone hurt." Sophy leaned over and refilled Sir George's cup, and placed a dish of macaroons near his hand.

He picked one up, nibbling at it absently, without ever realizing that she had the cook bake them for him especially. Sighing, he shook his head. "I can forgive her, perhaps, for rushing off so heedlessly, but that she should go with Lord Blackthorn is beyond my comprehension. Heaven only knows what Mother will say when she hears of this. I do not scruple to tell you, my dear, that she already thinks Lydia too . . ."

Sophy nodded as he searched for the appropriate word. "I quite understand what you mean, Sir George. I own I, too, am surprised that she would drive off with a gentleman she previously has held in positive aversion. Of course, I do not know Lord Blackthorn well, but on the few occasions we have met, he did not impress me at all favorably."

"Really? I am astonished to hear you say so. Most young ladies seem to find him perfection, and cannot sing his praises sufficiently."

Sophy laughed lightly. "Perhaps because I am older, I have higher standards. Certainly I will concede Lord Blackthorn to be handsome, for one cannot fault his features, but I find that he lacks those distinguishing manners that mark a true gentleman of refinement, such as yourself. Indeed, when he escorted me home from Vauxhall, I was quite ill at ease in his presence."

"My dear Miss Remfrey, I did not realize! I must offer you my apologies if through my fault you were thrown into company which—"

"That is entirely unnecessary, Sir George," she interrupted. "You must not think I mean to complain. Lord Blackthorn neither said nor did anything to which one could take exception. It was merely his demeanor, which I found somewhat forbidding. But there, I have become spoiled, so much am I in your company. With you, I am always quite comfortable."

He smiled warmly at her. "Thank you, my dear, and, of course, I return the compliment. We have become old friends, have we not? I own I sometimes wish that Lydia possessed your sense of decorum—not that she does not have lovely manners—but you have a way of making a gentleman feel . . . well, as though his opinion mattered."

"But of course it does," she assured him with patent sincerity. "Why, I know of no one whose advice or judgment I value more."

Much gratified, he said, "That is kind of you, but I fear Lydia does not share your sentiments. I would not say this to anyone else, but I sometimes feel that she is impatient with me and thinks my notions of propriety too old-fashioned. Perhaps she is right."

"Oh no, you must not believe that. Lydia does lack patience, but she knows that is one of her failings and she tries very hard to overcome it. 'Tis only that she wants things done at once, and it chafes her when she is forced to wait. She is needle-witted, too, and inclined to plunge ahead when a more prudent person would advise caution."

"A perfect example being this afternoon," Sir George said ruefully. "Her concern for the boy was commendable, but you, too, were in need of her assistance, and I cannot help thinking that a relative should take precedence over the claims of a mere stranger."

"True, dear sir, but I do believe this was an indication of the complete trust Lydia reposes in you. She did not spare more than a passing thought for me because she knew I was in your care and therefore would be perfectly looked after. Perhaps it was taking advantage of your kindness, but we have both come to rely on you so particularly that I am sure Lydia did not give it a second thought." She hesitated, then added, "I do hope I properly thanked you for coming to my assistance?"

"It was my pleasure," George replied in all truth, for it had made him feel good to come to her rescue.

She sighed. "I feel so foolish, nearly fainting at the mere sight of blood."

"Nonsense. Any lady with your exquisite sensibilities would feel the same, and you must never apologize for it. It is one of the traits that make you so charmingly feminine."

He laughed to cover his sudden embarrassment and reached for his cup the same instant Sophy did. As their hands touched, she glanced up at him. Such pretty eyes, Sir George thought. With a shock, he suddenly realized how attractive he found her.

Sophy quickly withdrew her hand and covered her confusion by rising. "I . . . I believe the tea must be cold. I shall ring for more and—"

He rose. "Please do not trouble yourself on my account. I really should leave. I'd not meant to stay for so long, but I thought to make certain Lydia returned safely. However, I must be keeping you from other engagements."

She smiled wryly. "I have none, sir, and if you would not think it too forward of me, I would be deeply grateful if you would remain. I am nearly certain no harm has come to Lydia, but one cannot help worrying."

"I am entirely at your service, Miss Remfrey," he responded, and tried to think of something clever to say to ease the concern in her eyes. He looked down at her, so tiny, so helpless, so much in need of a gentleman to guide her, and all his protective instincts were aroused. Without conscious thought, he took a step toward her, but halted at the sudden sound of voices in the hall.

Chapter 10

Lydia swept into the drawing room, her cheeks flushed from the carriage drive, and her hair disordered just enough so that it fell in a soft cloud about her face. Her green eyes sparkled, and with her lips slightly parted, she presented a vision of loveliness.

"Oh, Sir George, I am so glad you are here," she said as she approached him with her hand held out. "I particularly wished to thank you for seeing Aunt Sophy safely home, but, of course, I knew I could utterly rely on you."

His anger melted beneath the warmth of her gaze, and he pressed her hand. "I am always pleased to be of service to you, my dear."

Sophy stared in disbelief. She had known, of course, that Sir George would forgive her niece. He always did so. Still, she had expected him to censure Lydia's conduct, if only mildly. That he did not was another indication of the depth of his devotion to her.

The knowledge caused Sophia such a stab of disappointment that she turned to her niece and spoke more sternly than was her habit. "We were quite concerned, Lydia. Had not someone remarked that they'd seen you drive off with Lord Blackthorn, we would have had no notion of what had become of you. Nor was I in any condition to conduct a search for you. I believe you owe us both an apology."

"Oh, dear. I am truly sorry, Aunt Sophy. You must know I never meant to worry you, only that poor boy was so dreadfully hurt, I could not think of anything else. But tell me at once, how are you feeling?"

"Your concern is somewhat belated, but thank you for asking. As you can see, I am quite recovered, though that is due in large part to Sir George."

Both pleased and embarrassed, he protested, "I really did very little, though I am glad I was at hand."

Lydia agreed to it, apologized to them both again, then insisted her aunt be seated, and rang for fresh tea. Turning to George with a warm smile, she coaxed, "You are not leaving yet, I hope? Do, please, stay. I know you both will wish to hear what happened to Mr. Bellows."

When everyone was comfortably seated again and fresh tea had been poured, Lydia explained about the balloonist, his injuries, and the horrors of the hospital, concluding, "Of course, it will be some time before he can be moved, but I thought it most kind of Mr. Richmond to offer to house him."

"Extremely so," Sir George remarked. "Why, none of you really know a thing about this fellow. I cannot say I approve of your intention to visit him. Surely, now that you know he will be well cared for, you can put him from your mind."

"I think Sir George is right, Lydia," Sophy added. "No good can come of encouraging Mr. Bellows to feel he has a claim on your friendship. I realize your natural kindness led you to become involved to the extent you have, but do you not feel it would be wiser now to keep your distance?"

"We shall see," Lydia said, hiding the flare of resentment she felt. She had promised Harry Bellows she would visit him, and visit him she would, whether or not anyone else approved. To George, she said, "I do regret that Mr. Bellows's accident spoiled our afternoon."

He chuckled. "I am becoming accustomed to it! It appears our excursions are to be fraught with unexpected danger. Betwixt footpads and balloonists crashing into trees, one can only wonder what will happen next."

Lydia smiled dutifully. "Let us hope nothing out of the ordinary occurs at Lady Jersey's masquerade on Thursday—that is, if you are still willing to provide us escort?"

"Of course, my dear, but I shall hope to see you before then. Mother charged me to request the pleasure of your company for dinner on Wednesday, and you, too, Miss Remfrey. She begs you will forgive the informality of the invitation, but it will just be a small dinner, with family and a few friends."

Lydia did a rapid calculation. She had several plans for Wednesday, but none, she thought, that could not be either altered or canceled. If Lady Weymouth was offering an olive branch, it was important it be accepted. She nodded. "It sounds quite delightful, and we should be pleased to accept, would we not, Aunt Sophy?"

"Certainly, my dear, and 'tis most kind of Lady Weymouth to include me. Sir George, please be sure to convey my regards to her."

He promised to do so, but mention of his mother reminded him that she would have expected him home some time ago, and he rose to take his leave.

After he had left, Lydia slipped off her shoes and tucked her feet up beneath her. Smothering a yawn, she murmured, "Lord, what an exhausting day. I hope we have no guests for dinner?"

"Fortunately no, but we are committed to several engagements later. Lady Kathryn's rout is this evening, and we are promised to dear Verity Lynton—"

"Stop," Lydia pleaded, holding up her hand. "Let us have dinner first and recoup our strength. At the moment, the Prince Regent himself could not command my attendance, and you must be equally tired. Aunt Sophy, I must apologize again for leaving you today. At the time I thought I had good reasons, but you are right—it was extremely thoughtless of me. May I hope that you have forgiven me?"

Sophy sighed. "Of course, my dear. For myself, it does not matter, but I own I am disturbed to see you treat Sir George so cavalierly."

"Was he very angry?"

"No, not angry—disappointed, perhaps. I think it must be most humiliating for a gentleman to see the young lady he places first in his affections dismiss him with so little regard."

"But I did not!" Lydia protested, truly astonished that anyone would think such a thing.

Sophy's brows rose, and she gently reprimanded her niece. "I do not know what else you could call it when you abandoned him to go off without so much as a word of explanation, and accompanied only by Lord Blackthorn."

Daunted, Lydia rubbed her head, which was now aching fiercely. "I went with the boy, Aunt Sophy. I was concerned about him. Lord Blackthorn's presence had nothing to do with my decision, and I certainly would not place *him* above Sir George. You must know how I feel about Lord Blackthorn."

"I thought I did, but . . . to be honest, my dear, you appeared to be on the most intimate terms with him when you were tending that boy. I heard you call him by his Christian name, and your manner was hardly that of a young lady who holds him in aversion. Granted, my impression was fleeting, for I was near to fainting, but if I noticed so much, I am certain Sir George did, too."

Lydia sipped her tea. She was aware that for a short while she had slipped into the old intimacy she and Justin had once shared. It had seemed so natural to turn to him, and certainly she was grateful for his assistance, but for her aunt to think that she had valued him above Sir George was ludicrous.

She set her cup down and rose. "I think you forget that I was once engaged to Lord Blackthorn. Had I wished to do so, I could have wed him five years ago."

Sophy smiled ruefully as she, too, rose. "It is precisely that engagement I am remembering. You were attracted to the gentleman once, therefore, I do not believe it unreasonable to suppose you might be again. Now darling, do not frown at me for I do not mean to criticize you or censure your conduct. I only wish to make certain you know your own heart. If Sir George has truly engaged your affections, and you wish to wed him, I would be the first to wish you happy."

"But you have reservations," Lydia said, stung by her aunt's words.

"I do. It does not seem to me that you hold him in the proper esteem, and he is too fine a gentleman to trifle with his feelings. However, if you tell me otherwise—"

"My affections for Sir George have not changed," Lydia interrupted. "You are refining too much on a few words you chanced to overhear."

Sophy hugged her. "Then, there is no more to be said."

Lydia wished it were so simple. She went up to change her gown before dinner, but although she may have put an end to the discussion, she could not erase the memory of her aunt's words from her mind. They haunted her the next day, causing her to question her own motives, so that when she chanced to see Lord Blackthorn at Lady Granville's, she thought it prudent to try to avoid him.

She'd seen him the moment he entered the crowded salon, for it was impossible to mistake his tall, elegant figure. Through the shifting crowd, she caught glimpses of him. He wore a dark brown dress coat, with a cream-colored embroidered vest. Both were simply cut, plain by many standards, as was his white linen stock, but he was clearly the most impressive gentleman present, as was evidenced by the number of young ladies who tried to claim his attention.

Let them, Lydia thought, and prayed they would keep him occupied while she slipped out of the room. It might be cowardly of her, but with her aunt and Mrs.

Fullerton, Lady Weymouth's dear friend, both present and observing her every move, she thought it wisest.

She was nearly at the door when he suddenly appeared in front of her. "Lord, what a crush! How do you endure these affairs day after day?"

"Very easily, my lord. One must keep moving. Pray excuse me."

His eyes crinkled with amusement as he regarded her. "So haughty, Miss Osborne. Now, what have I done to unwittingly offend you?"

Conscious that her aunt was watching her from across the room, Lydia lifted her chin a fraction. "I am sure I do not know what you mean, my lord."

"You called me Justin yesterday."

Disconcerted, she stammered, "I . . . I should not have done so, but the . . . the circumstances were exceptional."

"I see," he said with a rakish grin.

He had cornered her in the salon, his tall frame securely blocking her way. He was quite capable of ignoring the other people milling about the room, and the dozens of eyes that gazed at them curiously. Unless she made a scene, she was trapped for the moment.

"Did I ever tell you how beautiful you look when you play the ice princess?" he asked, his vibrant voice pitched low.

"If that is meant as a compliment, I must tell you I find it in extremely poor taste. Do, pray, excuse me. I see my aunt is waiting for me."

He shifted slightly as she tried to step around him, effectively cutting off her escape. "She has not waited nearly as long as I, my sweet. Does this new facade of coolness mean you no longer wish to visit Mr. Bellows? It cheered him immensely when we told him you would call, but, of course, if you have had second thoughts, I am sure he will understand. What happened, Liddy? Did Sir George take exception to your excursion with me?"

"Sir George has nothing to do with my decision," she

retorted. "You know as well as I that I should never have accompanied you to the hospital. It was . . . it was wrong of me to go with you."

"By whose standards? The Liddy I knew would never allow anyone to dictate to her. *She* followed her heart, and the devil take the consequences."

She couldn't help the blush that crept up her cheeks, and whispered furiously, "The girl you knew, my lord, was very young and very foolish. Perhaps she has merely grown up."

He laughed hollowly. "If that is so, how exquisitely ironic that I should have waited for that event all these years only to discover that I quite dislike the results." He stepped aside and with a wave of his hand indicated she was free to pass. "I shall convey your regrets to Mr. Bellows. I am sure he will understand. After all, he is a mere commoner, and must realize you are a grand lady and quite above his touch."

As his words lashed her, the memory of the red-headed balloonist and his hopeful eyes bit at her conscience. She hesitated, then said, "I promised Mr. Bellows I would visit him, and I shall make arrangements with Perdita to do so. I always keep my promises."

"Not always, Liddy," he said beneath his breath as she swept past him.

Why did he have to come back to town now? Lydia fumed as she smiled vacantly at several ladies. She made her way to her aunt's side, and though she made every effort to concentrate on the conversation at hand, her eyes betrayed her. She watched Lord Blackthorn as he moved through the room, and felt wretchedly miserable when he disappeared through the double doors. Ridiculous, she told herself, to feel as though she had somehow disappointed him. She forced herself to concentrate on what Kathryn Delacourt was saying, inquired politely after the lady's brother and his new bride, but barely heard the response. Foolish it might be, but she could not erase the memory of the contempt she'd seen in Justin's eyes.

Perdita approached her a few moments later and whispered, "Fighting with my brother again? I saw him leaving, looking as black as a thundercloud."

Lydia, pretending indifference, murmured, "Why should you think I had anything to do with Justin's temper?"

"Because, my dearest, best of friends, you are the only one who has that effect on him." She drew Lydia into a recessed alcove where a small sofa provided a convenient seat for those desiring private conversation. "Now, tell me what has happened. I had hoped the pair of you were becoming friends again."

"I fear that is impossible. At the moment, he is annoyed merely because I had second thoughts about the advisability of visiting our balloonist, but I doubt that anything I do would please him."

Perdita patted her hand. "I agree he can be difficult, but then you both expect too much of each other."

Astonished, Lydia stared at her. "You are mistaken, 'Dita. I expect nothing of your brother save that he behave civilly when we meet."

"Really? Yet it seems to me you expect a great deal of him. Were you not furious with him when he would not seek out the gentleman who attacked your maid? And, at Vauxhall—does my memory plague me or were you not rather angry when he refused to chase after that footpad? And yesterday—am I mistaken, or would you not have been extremely disappointed if Justin had not gone to Harry Bellows's rescue?"

Lydia shook her head. "That was entirely different. Good heavens, 'Dita, would you not expect any gentleman who witnessed such an accident to do what he could to help?"

"Perhaps, but it was Justin you turned to. If you truly believe what you say, then I can only wonder why you did not request Cedric's assistance, or Sir George's, or Mr. Neville's, all of whom were present at the time."

"I will not discuss this any further," Lydia declared, unable to think clearly. She rose. "You are obviously biased and believe your brother to be beyond criticism."

Perdita stood as well and, in her soft, gentle voice, said sadly, "It is not I who carries a vision of Justin as some sort of knight on a white charger, but you, my dear. Since first you met, you have imagined him as the hero of all those silly books we used to read. No gentleman could live up to that, Lydia. But then, he is just as bad. He will never hear a word of criticism against you."

"I find that difficult to believe since he continually finds fault with me."

Perdita smiled. "That may be, my dear, but you may trust me when I tell you that Justin never allows anyone else to criticize you—not even me." She sighed. "Perhaps it is just as well you've quarreled again. Heaven knows, were you to wed, none of us would know a moment's peace."

The following morning, Lydia awoke early. She had spent a restless night, tormented by dreams that prominently featured a knight on a white charger. She awoke irritable, annoyed with herself for allowing her aunt and Perdita to trouble her thoughts with their ridiculous notions. She knew Justin for what he was—an arrogant, domineering, demanding male—and not at all the sort of gentleman she wanted for a husband. The beginning of a headache teased at the nerves behind her eyes.

Impatiently she rang for Finch and, when her maid appeared, demanded to know if she had so many other pressing duties that she could not find the time to bring her mistress a cup of chocolate and the mail.

The tall dresser bit back a retort. This was clearly not a morning when impertinences would be tolerated. She disappeared, returning in a matter of moments with a tray laden with a pot of chocolate, a delicate china cup and saucer, fresh flowers, and a four-inch-high stack of letters. After settling the tray on her mistress's lap, and drawing open the curtains, she discreetly withdrew.

Lydia smothered a yawn and rifled the stack of letters. They were predictably the same as she received every day, with only one or two exceptions. She smiled as she read a sweet note from Miss Gilbert thanking her for the invitation to Vauxhall Gardens.

Several invitations were carelessly tossed aside, a letter from an old friend extolling the virtues of marriage and motherhood followed, but Lydia's attention was arrested when she caught sight of an elegant envelope bearing her mother's distinctive script.

Lady Claire Osborne wrote only when a matter of supreme urgency or importance required her to do so. She admitted she was a terrible correspondent. While she could speak fluently on any number of wide-ranging topics, and was always at ease with strangers, she found putting words down on paper extremely difficult and confining.

With a tremor of concern, Lydia slit open the envelope and withdrew the heavy vellum stationery, quickly scanning the crossed and recrossed lines. Sir Matthew, her mother had written, was going to drive himself into an early grave if something were not done, and she was at her wits' end. Dr. Longfellow had ordered him to bed, but, of course, her father in his usual stubborn manner had refused to comply and, despite the pains he'd suffered in his chest, insisted on resuming his normal duties on the estate.

While she saw no cause for immediate alarm, Lady Claire wrote that she hoped her daughter would return home for a visit at the end of the Season. Perhaps she would be able to exert some influence over her father and persuade him to allow the estate manager to take over some of the more arduous duties.

Lydia sighed. Her papa was the worst patient in the world. Nothing distressed him more than being laid low with an illness, and Mama was of little help. It worried her when he was sick, and because she fretted, she tended to nag at him to take care of himself, which only made him the more stubborn. The moment he was told he could not do something, he became determined to do it. It was one trait they shared in common.

She smiled remembering the time two years ago when Sir Matthew had been laid up with the gout. She had gone home that year, too, in answer to a desperate plea from her mother. Papa could be a bear when he was ill. Before her arrival, he had threatened to turn off half the staff, quarreled with most of the neighbors, and reduced Mama to tears.

No one had been able to reason with him except Lydia. Perhaps because she was their only child, born when they had lost hope of ever having children, Sir Matthew cherished an exceptionally soft spot in his heart for his daughter. He had never been able to deny her anything, not the pony she'd coveted at four, or new dresses at fourteen, or putting her hair up at sixteen.

Mama said Lydia had a way of looking at him as though her heart were breaking, which turned Sir Matthew to mush. Lydia knew it to be true, and she was not above occasionally using the knowledge to her advantage, or for her father's own good. She would see what she could do to put him back in frame. The Season would be over in a few weeks. She laid her mother's letter aside, planning to answer it later, and made a note to ask Aunt Sophy if she'd like to come with her to Maidstone at the end of the Season.

Finch tapped lightly on the door, then poked her head in. "Are you ready to dress now, miss?"

"I am, and you may safely come in, Finch. I am sorry if I bit your head off this morning."

"That's all right, miss," the tall dresser said as she crossed the room and opened the wardrobe. "We all have our moods now and then, and from what the other maids say, you're better 'an most to work for."

"How reassuring, but do try to contain your enthusiasm," Lydia answered dryly.

132

Finch grinned at her as she held out two walking dresses for Lydia's inspection.

"I think the apricot with the matching pelisse," Lydia decided as she rose and stretched. "And the new straw hat," she added, strolling to her dressing table. Her mind was already on the day ahead. She had morning calls to pay, an engagement to drive in the park with the Duke of Lansing, who apparently had something of importance he wished to discuss with her, and then when she returned, it would be time to dress for dinner with Sir George and his mother.

Lydia studied her reflection in the looking glass as nerves twisted her stomach into unaccustomed and unpleasant knots. Once she would have relished such a schedule, but this morning she only found the prospect tiresome. Perhaps it was the knowledge that her father was ill, or just a sudden bout of homesickness, but she suddenly wished she were back home at Stone's End.

The river gardens would be in bloom, she thought, and she could walk down to the Little Bridge at the foot of Gabriel's Hill without a maid or footman, and no one would think twice about it.

She tried to envision Sir George there, striding about the grounds of Stone's End with her papa, taking an interest in the corn crop or the apple groves, but the image would not come to life. As she leaned back in the chair so Finch could brush out her hair, she wondered what her father would think of Sir George. Although Papa had said little, Lydia knew he'd been deeply disappointed when she broke off her betrothal to Justin Lambert.

Sir Matthew had admired the younger man and, much to Lydia's astonishment, had sided with Justin when he'd refused to resign his commission and marry her at once. Papa had said Justin's loyalty to his regiment was commendable, a pronouncement that still rankled. She, however, had seen Justin's insistence on postponing their wedding a year as proof that he did not care as much as she did, for she had found the idea of waiting so long unbearable. But despite all her tears and pleas, Justin had refused to reconsider his decision.

And he was still just as stubborn, as autocratic, as dictatorial—and she could be thankful that the betrothal had come to nothing. She was well out of it, she thought. She would wed a gentleman who considered *her* feelings, and who could be counted on to put *her* desires first.

Thinking of Sir George, she decided that if all went well at dinner tonight, she might ask him to provide her escort home. It would give him an opportunity to meet her parents and see something of Maidstone. Fond as she was of London, Lydia fully intended to settle near her parents. She loved Kent, and Stone's End would be hers one day.

She was roused from her musing as her aunt rushed into her room. "Lydia? You will never believe—" Sophy broke off her words abruptly as she realized her niece was not alone. "Finch, would you leave us for a moment, please?"

"Aunt Sophy, what on earth has you in such a flutter?" Lydia asked as her maid discreetly withdrew.

Sophy waited until the door clicked shut, then hurried across the room to take Lydia's hand in hers. "I have heard the most amazing rumor, my dear, and I thought you should hear it from me. You will not credit it, but it appears that Lord Blackthorn has run off with Miss Piedmore!"

Chapter 11

Lydia sat motionless, feeling as though the breath had been squeezed from her lungs. Then rational thought returned and she inhaled deeply. Withdrawing her hand from her aunt's, she managed a nervous laugh and turned to face the looking glass. "Heavens, do not tell me you believe anything so patently ridiculous? The very notion is absurd."

Slightly affronted, Sophy sniffed and seated herself on the brocade love seat. "Then, perhaps you can explain why Miss Piedmore and Lord Blackthorn are both missing from their homes this morning."

"There could be any number of reasons, if, indeed, there is any truth to the rumor that neither is at home." Lydia glanced at the mantel clock and added, "It is only half-past ten. Where had you this gossip so early?"

"Lucy, Mrs. Barrows's niece who helps in the kitchen, is cousin to one of Mrs. Lambert's housemaids, and she saw her at the market this morning. According to Lucy, the Lamberts' household is in an uproar. His lordship was in a black mood when he left yesterday, and he has yet to return."

"I see, and from that tidbit you deduced he must have eloped with Cynthia Piedmore? Really, Aunt Sophy, I am surprised you could be so credulous. Lord Blackthorn may have left town to take in a prizefight, or perhaps he spent the night at his club, having, as gentlemen do, indulged in too much drink."

"But no one has seen him," Sophy insisted. "And he had an engagement to look in at Tattersall's with Mr.

Richmond this morning, which is when it was discovered that he never slept in his bed. Lucy said dear Mrs. Lambert is quite prostrate with worry."

"I very much doubt that. I know Mrs. Lambert, and she is a most sensible lady. Good heavens, Aunt Sophy, even when her son was wounded, and I was present when she received the news, she did not take to her bed. Nor is she unaccustomed to Lord Blackthorn spending the night away from home. Have you forgotten he was in the military, and for five years has maintained his own household?"

"But to see one's only son make a misalliance, compounded by the scandal of an elopement, that, my dear Lydia, is a very different matter and sufficient to grieve any mother. And when I tell you that Miss Piedmore left a letter for her mother, apologizing for doing that which must place her beyond the pale—well, I can only say that if you do not choose to believe the rumors, you are the only one!"

"Miss Piedmore left a letter?" Lydia asked, trying not to allow the doubt she suddenly felt creep into her voice.

"She did," Sophy confirmed. "Although her parents are giving out that she has suddenly gone to Bath to visit her ailing grandmother, a housemaid found the missive when she went to turn the bed down last evening. Of course the girl couldn't read, but Mrs. Piedmore nearly fainted when the letter was carried to her and that tells its own tale."

Lydia rose and pulled the bell for Finch as she told her aunt, "Nonsense. Even if Miss Piedmore eloped, what makes you think she did so with Lord Blackthorn? Certainly her parents would not object to that marriage."

"They may not, but the Lamberts most assuredly would. And 'tis rumored he was drinking heavily last evening. Perhaps she persuaded him to elope with her when he was in his cups."

136

Finch tapped on the door and stepped in. "Are you ready for me now, miss?"

Lydia nodded. "Pray, excuse me, Aunt Sophy. I must dress, but I promise you I shall see Perdita today and find out the truth of the matter. In the meantime, I pray you will not speak of this."

With that, Sophy had to be content. They talked for a few more minutes, discussing the evening engagements, but at last she withdrew, allowing Lydia to dress.

The moment the door shut, Finch said, "I wouldn't paid no heed to that tale, miss. That Lucy—she's just a scullery maid and never gets her stories straight—"

"Enough," Lydia interrupted. "I have told you before that I will not tolerate anyone eavesdropping outside my door."

Unabashed, Finch carefully placed the straw bonnet on Lydia's hair. "Yes, miss, and I wouldn't, but I couldn't help overhearing, waiting as I was by the door in case you needed me. You know I wouldn't listen on purpose, but Miss Remfrey's voice kind of carries like."

Lydia sighed. Arguing was useless, but there were other methods effective in controlling her maid's impertinence. She curtly informed Finch she would not require her attendance, left instructions regarding the dresses she would require later, and then summoned a footman to order her carriage brought around from the mews.

Perdita was waiting when she arrived, attractively dressed and in excellent spirits. Nor was there any sign of anything amiss in the Lambert household. Far from being prostrate, Mrs. Lambert greeted Lydia cordially, inquired after her family, and asked to be remembered to Miss Remfrey. Her demeanor was much as usual, and Lydia could detect no sign of worry as Mrs. Lambert walked them to the door, fondly kissed them both, and urged them to mind their manners.

Once in the privacy of the carriage, Perdita grinned impishly. "I can see you have heard the rumors, but are much too well-bred to ask if there's any truth in them."

"Not in front of your mother," Lydia replied with a smile. "I am amazed at how well she looks, for the gossips have it that she is prostrate with worry."

Perdita laughed. "Mama has better sense than to get in a dither merely because Justin chose not to come home one night. It is not the first time, and I very much doubt it will be the last."

"Then, that much was true? You have not seen him today?"

Perdita shook her head, her dark curls dancing, an amused light in her eyes. "No, but there is nothing in that to alarm one, and if it were not for Miss Piedmore eloping, no one would think twice about it."

No more could be said as the carriage halted in front of Lady Compton's, and the footman was at the door to let the steps down. As the ladies entered the house, Perdita linked her arm through her friend's, tilted up her chin and whispered, "Ready for the inquisition?"

"Surely no one will be bold enough to question you directly."

"Oh no. We shall only have to deal with sly innuendos and subtle hints. I would have stayed at home, only that would have fueled the gossip. Oh, good afternoon, Mrs. Parnel . . ."

Perdita proved correct in her predictions. They stayed only twenty minutes, and although no mention of the rumors were made directly, more than a dozen ladies solicitously inquired after her family, particularly of Lord Blackthorn. Perdita answered them all with sunny smiles, and replied her brother was quite well, thank you.

Miss Fredericka Martin, perhaps more audacious than the rest, approached Lydia and inquired sweetly if she had heard that Miss Piedmore had eloped. "The news is all over town, my dear, but the question is, with whom did she fly to Gretna Green? I thought it might have been Mr. Neville, but he was seen in town this morning, quite crushed by the news."

Lydia, her brows angling upward, answered with a

show of wide-eyed astonishment, "But did Miss Piedmore elope? *I* heard that she is in Bath, visiting her ailing grandmother."

"So her family is saying, but it will not wash—not when her maid was seen crying buckets of tears and moaning that her poor dear mistress was ruined. I ask you, does that sound as though she is visiting Bath?"

"I do not put much credence in rumors, Miss Martin. You may take it from one who has been in town for several years, that more than half the gossip one hears is utterly without substance."

Miss Martin looked ready to disagree, but Perdita interrupted their tête-à-tête, reminding Lydia that it was time they took their leave.

When they were safely in the carriage, Lydia fumed, "It is worse than I imagined. The tattle-mongers have it that Felix Neville is devastated and drowning his sorrow in brandy at Boodle's. Mrs. Parnel told me Alexander Saunders was seen this morning, sporting a black eye, and there are any number of tales about Miss Piedmore's maid, and if only half of them are true, she must be an incredibly stupid girl."

Perdita agreed to it, but thought her no more foolish than Miss Piedmore, who'd left such an ambiguous letter that all manner of conjecture could be drawn. "I do not believe for an instant that Justin eloped with her—the very notion is ludicrous—but, oh, I do wish he would return home and put a stop to all this gossip."

Lydia patted her hand. Hoping she sounded more reassuring than she felt, she said, "Perhaps by the time we finish our calls, he will be at home. I imagine he will be much amused to know the speculation he has caused."

Justin stepped wearily down from the carriage and checked his pocket watch. Ten o'clock. He'd made the drive from Barnet, just north of London, to Bath in a record-setting nine hours. 'Twas small wonder his shoulders and arms ached like the devil, and he still had the return trip to London before him.

He strode to the carriage and opened the door. Cynthia Piedmore laid curled up on one seat as fast asleep as a babe, though traces of the copious amount of tears she'd shed earlier still streaked her face. On the seat opposite, the abigail he'd hired at the King's Arms slumped against the squabs and snoring lustily.

"Ladies, we have arrived," Justin said, and when neither stirred, reached in and shook the abigail's arm.

She came to with a start, blinked at him owlishly, then recollected that she'd been engaged to travel with the young lady to Bath. "Have we arrived, then?" she asked, trying to smother a yawn.

"We have. Please wake Miss Piedmore, and then see her safely inside." He pressed some notes into her hand. "There's ample here for your stagecoach fare back to Barnet, and then some to compensate you for your trouble."

"Thank you, sir," the gangly girl trilled, her eyes boggling at the small fortune she held in her hands. "It weren't no trouble," she protested, but quickly stuffed the notes into her reticule.

While his lordship stretched his long legs outside the carriage, she gently nudged the young lady. Her charge would not be deemed pretty under any circumstances, but with her eyes all red and her face splotched from crying, she presented such a pathetic picture that Annie wondered at her involvement with his lordship. She glanced out the window. He was a handsome one, even with his coat dirtied and torn and the tiredness in those devilish blue eyes that she'd seen turn to ice if anyone dared gainsay him.

And handy with his dukes, she thought, remembering the way he'd floored the other gentleman. But what puzzled her was why the pair of them had engaged in fisticuffs over the likes of Miss Piedmore. It was usually the pretty ones that had the gentlemen brawling.

Outside the carriage, Justin was wondering much the same thing. It was no business of his what Miss Piedmore did, only he'd had the misfortune to be in the

King's Arms when Saunders had brought her inside. No one could have ignored the commotion, and Justin had glanced around curiously. He'd recognized her at once. She was obviously frightened and near to hysterics, and although Saunders had bespoken a private parlor, the girl's terrified wails had penetrated to the taproom.

Justin downed his ale and told himself it was no concern of his. He had his own problems. Annoyed with Lydia, he'd drunk more than he should have and worked himself into a rage. Unfit company for anyone, he'd taken the reins, dismissed his groom, and driven his carriage north, pushing himself and his team until he'd worked off his fury. It had taken him as far as Barnet.

When he saw Saunders stride outside, Justin sighed, drained his tankard, and crossed to the door leading to the private parlor. He tapped gently, then called, "Miss Piedmore? Are you in trouble?"

The sounds of muffled sobbing ceased, and a second later the door flew open. Cynthia Piedmore, tears running down her cheeks, stared at him and sobbed, "Lord Blackthorn! Oh, please, sir, I don't deserve that you should, but I beg you to help me."

If only women wouldn't weep, Justin thought, and wished for Lydia. They'd had some rousing quarrels, and she might rant and rave at him, but she'd never resorted to tears, thank God. It unnerved him to see a lady cry, turned his knees to jelly and his iron will to pudding. He withdrew his handkerchief and shoved it into the girl's hands. "I'll do whatever I can, Miss Piedmore, but we can accomplish nothing if you don't cease crying and tell me what's amiss."

"Oh, I have been so foolish, so wicked," she moaned. "If only I had it to do over again!"

Justin sighed, awkwardly patted her shoulder, and tried to urge her to make sense. His own senses were still slightly befuddled by brandy. "What have you done? Why are you here?"

She looked up to tell him, saw the gentleman enter

141

behind him, and wailed, "Oh, please, Lord Blackthorn, do not abandon me."

Saunders stepped into the room, slamming the door shut behind him. "This is none of your affair, my lord, and I suggest you leave at once."

"It appears the lady has other notions, Saunders. If I leave, I take her with me."

"Do not be hasty, my lord. I think you cannot understand the situation. Miss Piedmore agreed to elope with me. We, as you no doubt have guessed, are on our way to Gretna Green. I assure you she was quite willing, but the tedious drive has preyed upon her nerves. She is merely suffering a fit of the vapors and will be better directly, particularly if you will be so good as to leave us alone."

Justin stared at him, contempt in his eyes. "I'd heard you lost your fortune. Is this how you mean to recoup it? Only a scoundrel would force a lady to elope."

The blow Saunders aimed landed swiftly, catching Justin on the shoulder, but he returned it with a deadly right that promised Saunders a blackened eye on the morrow.

Driving coats were rapidly shed, the tables and chairs shoved back, and the two men circled. Miss Piedmore alternated between watching helplessly and closing her eyes as she screamed. The innkeeper strode in, followed by the few travelers who'd been in the taproom. His knowing eye measured the situation, and he decided not to interfere. Havoc might ensue, but the tall fellow was a gentleman by the looks of him, and he'd pay for any damage he caused. The deciding factor was that it looked to be a good mill, and bets were already being laid.

Lord Blackthorn was the taller of the pair, and his arms had a longer reach, but Saunders was at least a stone heavier. For a time it appeared they were evenly matched, and the wagering favored first one, then the other. Justin was knocked off his feet once, shook his head and came up fighting mad. His blue eyes glim-

142

mered with an icy coldness, and taut muscles rippled beneath his shirt. With deadly precision, he landed a succession of steady blows, relentlessly backing his opponent into a corner. A right to the eye drew blood, and a left uppercut put Saunders out on the floor.

A rousing cheer went up. Justin, who'd been oblivious to the men that had crowded into the room, looked around in surprise. Someone handed him his coat, and he withdrew a sheaf of notes and tossed them to the innkeeper. "I believe this will cover any damage, and please be so good as to set up a round of drinks for everyone."

Another cheer followed, and the room rapidly emptied. With Saunders out cold, Justin turned his attention to Miss Piedmore. She had swooned at the sight of drawn blood, and the innkeeper's eldest daughter, Annie, had been sent in to tend her.

Remembering, Justin grimaced. Once the lady recovered, he'd eventually gotten the story out of her. In a long, drawn-out account, filled with dramatic cries, and punctuated by heartrendering sobs, she'd told him how Saunders had persuaded her to elope. He had paid court to her, writing her poetry and showering her with gifts until he'd convinced her that he loved her beyond all else. But they had both known her parents would never agree to the match. In desperation, Saunders had persuaded her to fly to Gretna Green.

"It was wrong of me, my lord," Miss Piedmore tearfully confessed. "I felt it in my heart when I wrote Mama begging her forgiveness, but it . . . it seemed so craven to withdraw then. But I wish I had, oh, I do so wish I had. And in the carriage—it was horrid. I knew I could not go through with the elopement, and I begged and begged to be taken home, but Mr. Saunders would not listen. And now . . . what am I to do? I am ruined!"

Justin felt the tiniest twinge of sympathy for the unconscious Saunders. Had it been him, he would have taken the girl home at once. Anything to avoid her tears. As they started flowing again, he tried to reassure her all was not lost.

The brandy had been the innkeeper's notion. Just a shot, he'd suggested, to calm the lady. Fortunately it had worked, and Justin had managed to pry the location of Miss Piedmore's nearest relative—apparently her grandmother—out of the girl. He didn't see what else could be done, save drive her to Bath and send a messenger to town to warn her parents not to spread the alarm.

And he had made excellent time, stopping only to change his teams. The brandy had calmed Miss Piedmore sufficiently that she'd fallen asleep after only a few miles, and dozed fitfully the rest of the way. It was just as well, he thought, for if anyone had seen her in his carriage, the fat would be in the fire, abigail or no.

"Lord Blackthorn?"

He turned as Miss Piedmore stepped from the carriage. Her lips trembling, she gazed mistily up at him. "I do not know how to thank you, my lord. It was extraordinarily kind of you to drive me here."

He smiled, trying to set her at ease. "No gentleman could do less, but I hope this will serve as a lesson to you not to go running off with the next man who tries to persuade you to do so."

Tears pooled in her eyes. "I . . . I doubt I shall ever be asked again. My conduct has placed me beyond the pale, and when word reaches London . . . the scandal"— she gulped as a sob escaped her lips.

Justin silently groaned. Lord, one would think the woman had no more tears within her, but it seemed as though she had an endless supply. He tried to stem the flow. "Try not to worry, Miss Piedmore. I sent a messenger to your parents, and by now they will know you are with your grandmother. They will give it out that she took sudden sick, and wished for your attendance. You bide here a fortnight or so, and then, if she is able, have your grandmother come back to town with you. That will put paid to any rumors."

"I do not deserve such consideration," she said, dabbing at the tears in her eyes. "How can I ever thank you?"

"You just let the abigail take you on inside, and rest a bit. I shall expect to see you looking as pretty as ever when you return to town, and if I am not much mistaken, there's another gentleman who will be extremely pleased to see you return."

She blushed, and held out her hand. "Will you not come in? Grandmother will wish to thank you as well, and I am sure you must be dreadfully tired. If you wish to rest—"

"Thank you," he interrupted, anxious to be on his way, "but I shall rack up at the Ship's Inn for an hour or two, and then I must get back to London." He drove off a few minutes later, and in less than a quarter hour, was pulling off his boots. He stretched out on the bed at the inn, drowsily remembering that he'd promised Cedric to look in at Tattersall's with him that morning. An arm thrown over his eyes, Justin's last thought before falling asleep was that Cedric was a good lad, and too sensible to worry . . .

Lydia smiled at the gentleman seated on her left. Mr. Phineas Bostwick, Sir George's uncle, had recently celebrated his seventieth birthday. Lean of figure, he was spry and had a roguish gleam in his small blue eyes. Unfortunately he was hard of hearing, and she had repeated three times that she found Mr. Poole's latest novel entertaining.

"Raining out, you say?" he boomed. "Well, 'tis to be expected we have showers this time of year."

She agreed to it, although the evening was warm and clear.

"I did warn you that you were wasting your time talking to Uncle Phineas," the young gentleman on her right smugly remarked. "He cannot hear a word you say."

Lydia sighed. She had done her best to put Mr.

Claude Ebert, Sir George's young nephew, in his place, but he seemed impervious to subtle hints. Aspiring to the dandy set, he was elegantly if somewhat garishly attired in a well-cut blue coat, a blinding blue-and-yellow waistcoat, an impossibly high collar that precluded his turning his neck more than an inch or two, and an elaborately tied stock. He obviously carried a very high opinion of himself, and showed no respect for his elders.

"It does make conversation rather difficult," she agreed, pointedly sampling the capon set before her.

"You need not worry. Uncle Phineas approves of any young lady who is passably pretty—and you, Miss Osborne, are certainly more than that." He winked at her, nudging her knee with his own.

Lydia had sufficient experience with such would-be rakes to know how to handle him. Smiling sweetly, she said, "Thank you, Mr. Ebert, but I believe I prefer the company of a deaf old man to an impertinent schoolboy who has not yet learned company manners. Touch me again, and I shall scream."

He choked on a sip of wine, and she turned her attention to Mr. Bostwick, praying that the interminable dinner would soon be over. Lady Weymouth was seated at the foot of the table, and observing Lydia's every move, no doubt hoping she would commit some dreadful faux pas. Sir George sat at the head of the table, too far away for conversation, and Aunt Sophy was on the opposite side, engaged in an animated discussion with another of Sir George's uncles.

Her aunt seemed to be enjoying herself, but Lydia was having difficulty concentrating. Perdita had promised to send her word if Justin returned, and Lydia had fully expected to hear that he had wandered home, none the worse for wear, and with some improbable tale of how he'd spent the evening. She would not have been at all surprised to learn he had dallied away the time with an actress or member of the demi monde. Only the message had never arrived.

146

Lydia sipped her wine, annoyed with herself for allowing Justin to occupy her thoughts to such an extent. She had even experienced a pang of jealousy at the thought of his eloping with Miss Piedmore. Odd, but she had never envisioned Justin as married, and she found the idea unsettling.

"Might I inquire where you are from, Miss Thorne?" Mr. Bostwick asked loudly, reclaiming her attention.

Lydia had given up correcting him on her name, and replied with a smile, "From Maidstone, sir."

"Marleybone? Ah, I know it well, but I do not recollect any Thornes . . ."

Lady Weymouth rose, signaling the other ladies that it was time to withdraw to the salon. With relief, Lydia smiled at Mr. Bostwick, then followed the other ladies up the stairs. In the overheated salon, she chose a seat near the windows, sitting down next to a young lady she had met briefly before dinner.

"Miss Fabersham, is it? I am Miss Osborne. Did I understand Lady Weymouth to say you are Sir George's cousin? I wonder we have not met before."

The girl smiled shyly at her. "I am not yet out. Mama allowed me to attend this evening because only family would be present—excepting you and Miss Remfrey, of course. She said it would be good practice for me."

"Well, I am delighted to be part of your unofficial presentation, though it is a pity that your first dinner should be such a . . . such an unexceptional affair." About to say dull, Lydia had quickly amended her words, then asked, "Are you staying with Lady Weymouth?"

Miss Fabersham shook her light brown curls. "Oh no. Mama would not wish to be so beholden. We are only here this evening because Lady Weymouth wished the family to meet you."

Their conversation was interrupted as, one by one, the other ladies of the family approached, spoke to Lydia briefly, and then withdrew. It was clear they had been told Sir George was thinking of offering for her,

147

and she was being judged. Lydia stifled an inane desire to stand up, spread her arms, and turn slowly so that they could have a proper look. She'd seen horses given less thorough inspections.

Fortunately the gentlemen did not linger over their brandy and cigars, no doubt on Lady Weymouth's instructions, but filed into the room before Lydia said or did anything rash. Sir George crossed to her side at once.

"I think dinner went rather well," he pronounced with a satisfied air as he took the chair beside her. "Uncle Phineas said you were a charming girl, an assessment with which, of course, I heartily agree."

"Thank you," she murmured dutifully, waving her fan vainly in an effort to circulate the air. The room was stifling, and Lady Weymouth was of the school that believed night air hazardous to one's health, so there was small chance anyone would open a window. She glanced at Sir George, who seemed perfectly comfortable. Of course, he had grown up in this house. She had a sudden, daunting vision of sitting in this room in twenty years' time, arguing with George over whether or not the window should be open. She blinked, dismissing the image as the result of nerves.

Lady Weymouth rose, instantly claiming the attention of the room, but it was to Lydia she spoke. "My dear Miss Osborne, being new to one of our family gatherings, you will not be aware of one of our traditions, but we customarily enjoy a little music after dinner. The ladies take turns performing on the spinet, or giving us a song. I think it only fitting, since you are our guest, that you be invited to play the first song."

"Thank you, Lady Weymouth, but I am quite out of practice, and would much prefer to simply listen."

"Now, you must not be shy, my dear. As I said, you are among family, and I assure you that we are not overly critical. George, do persuade her."

"It would give me great pleasure to hear you sing," he said obligingly and offered his hand to assist her up.

148

Miss Fabersham unwittingly added her persuasion. "Oh, do please sing, Miss Osborne. I should so much like to hear you."

Lydia resolutely shook her head. "I really have no voice to speak of, and my performance on the spinet is mediocre at best."

George believed she was merely being modest and gazed at her fondly. "You must allow us to be the judge. Come, my dear, I will not take no for an answer."

"I am afraid you shall have to, as I do not intend to either sing or play the spinet," Lydia retorted, her patience wearing thin. "Pray, ask someone else."

The silence that suddenly fell in the room was deafening. Sophy rose suddenly and laid a hand on Sir George's arm. "If you will permit me, I would be pleased to perform in place of my niece."

Relieved, George agreed to it, but his shock at Lydia's tone, his disappointment that she should be so disobliging was obvious. Nor could he set her conduct down to a becoming modesty or a sudden shyness at performing in public. Not Miss Osborne, who had reigned over the *ton* for so many years.

He accompanied Miss Remfrey to the spinet, turned the pages for her as she sang a ballad in her soft, sweet voice, and remained beside her for the rest of the evening.

Chapter 12

Conversation during the drive home was polite, if somewhat strained. Lydia could barely wait to escape from the carriage, and welcomed their arrival in Bedford Square with considerable relief. She made no effort to detain Sir George, but bid him a pleasant good evening. Sophy was more effusive in expressing her gratitude for what she termed a delightful evening, a piece of fiction that had Lydia raising her brows in disbelief.

Applewood met them at the door, and when he had shut it upon Sir George, Lydia immediately demanded to know if she had received any messages during her absence.

"Yes, miss. A footman brought 'round a letter from Miss Lambert not an hour past. I took the liberty of placing it in your bedchamber."

"Thank you, Applewood," she replied, and turned eagerly toward the stairs.

"Lydia!" Sophy protested. "Are you simply retiring? Do you not feel that you owe me some explanation for your appalling behavior this evening? I must tell you that I was extremely embarrassed, and I know Sir George was mortified."

Lydia sighed and turned back. Noticing Applewood lingering in the hall, she gave him leave to retire and suggested to her aunt that they speak in the drawing room. She had long suspected her butler heard more than he let on. Sophy followed her in, disapproval emanating from her like a cloud of smoke from the fireplace.

Lydia firmly shut the door, then faced her aunt. "What would you have me say?"

Sophy, who hated confrontations of any sort and would never speak out on her own behalf, was righteously indignant for Sir George. "I must say I do not understand your attitude, Lydia. Do you not realize how churlishly you behaved this evening? I should be pleased to think there was some excuse for your conduct."

"Would you accept that I was tired?" Lydia asked, sinking into one of the giltwood chairs. "I found the entire evening tedious beyond belief and to be pressed to perform when I clearly did not wish to tried the limits of my patience. Sir George should have had better sense."

"I must disagree with you," Sophy declared. Too agitated to remain seated, she paced across the pale blue Axminster carpet. "Surely it would not have hurt you to play one song? After Sir George did you the honor of inviting you to meet his family—an honor which, I might add, you do not seem to appreciate in the least—" Lydia's trill of laughter interrupted her, and she stared at her niece aghast. "I cannot believe you find this amusing."

"And I cannot believe you find an evening such as this cause for appreciation. If it was an honor, I can only pray Sir George will spare me such distinction in the future. You may have enjoyed the dinner, Aunt Sophy, but enduring two very unpleasant hours seated between a young coxcomb who continuously went beyond the line and an older gentleman who could not hear one in three words I said is not my notion of pleasure."

Despite herself, Sophy's lips twitched. It had been a dreadful dinner, but that was hardly the point. She sat down in the chair next to her niece and took her hand. "I was referring to your behavior in the drawing room. My dear, do you not realize how you embarrassed Sir George? He said very little, but I can tell you he was not at all pleased, and one cannot blame him. The tone of voice you used—" she broke off, shaking her head. "I cannot think it well-done of you."

Lydia withdrew her hand. "I am sorry if I displeased you, Aunt Sophy, and I shall apologize to Sir George on the morrow. Does that satisfy you?"

Sophy studied her, a sad look in her eyes. "Do you not care for him at all?"

"Of course I do," Lydia said as she stood, "but he placed me in an impossible position. Believe me, it would have embarrassed him a great deal more had I obliged him and performed."

"I do not understand—"

Lydia bent and kissed her aunt's brow. "No, I can see you do not, and I shall have to confess. The sad truth is I can neither sing nor play the spinet. I am tone-deaf."

Sophy stared in disbelief. "But . . . but I am sure I must have heard you play—"

Lydia shook her head. "Never. I have not touched a spinet or opened my mouth to sing in public in more than a dozen years. I take great care not to, for I have no wish to be humiliated."

"Oh, my dear, I had no idea! But you must tell Sir George. I am certain that once he understands—"

"No!" Lydia interrupted. "This is not something I wish to discuss with anyone, and I hope you will respect my wishes. I will apologize to Sir George, but I intend to merely tell him that performing in public makes me uncomfortable—which it certainly does."

Sophy sighed. "Of course, if you wish it, I shall say nothing, but . . . oh, dear, it just seems to me that keeping such a secret from the gentleman one intends to wed indicates a lack of trust in a relationship which of necessity must be close. Are you quite certain that is wise?"

"I am not certain of anything tonight, save that I wish for my bed." After promising to think over her aunt's words, Lydia took her leave and wearily climbed the stairs to her bedchamber. But tired as she was, she immediately crossed to the secretary, and found Perdita's letter.

Sitting down, she opened the envelope and hastily read the neatly written missive. When she finished, fury flared in her eyes. She read the letter again, more slowly, then crumpled the paper and angrily tossed it into the fireplace.

She should have known it was foolish to worry over the likes of his lordship. While she had fretted, allowed concern for him to ruin a perfectly good day, Justin had been out carousing. Perdita had written he'd returned home late in the evening, dead on his feet, and in such a disreputable state, she would not be at all surprised to learn he had been in a brawl.

Lydia retrieved the ball of paper, smoothed it out, and read the latter portion again. "Of course, being Justin, he refused to answer any questions, would not say at all where he had been, except that something unexpected had occurred that had taken him out of town.

"Naturally I told him of the rumors circulating, at which he laughed heartily and said that only a sapscull would believe such a tale, and that when he married it would be done in style, which I hope I may live to see, but very much doubt. Having been parted from my brother for a number of years, I quite forgot how extremely annoying he can be. I fear I lost all patience when, after telling him that my dear Cedric had been worried as well, he replied that he was surprised, for he had thought Cedric possessed better sense.

"I must also tell you that before he retired, Justin inquired if you, my dearest Lydia, believed the rumors. I replied that I believed not, which seemed to please him, and he said he would call on you on the morrow."

There was more, but Lydia had read sufficient. Using the taper, she allowed the edge of the paper to catch flame, and then tossed it in the grate. When nothing but ashes remained, she rang for Finch. She paid scant attention to her maid's chatter as she prepared for bed, saying only that she was too sleepy for idle conversation. But sleep was long in coming, and not once did she think of Sir George.

Lydia had no intention of being at home when Lord Blackthorn called. She rose early, dressed and joined her aunt in the breakfast room as the clock chimed ten. "Good morning, Aunt Sophy. It looks to be a lovely day, does it not?"

Sophy glanced at her niece in surprise. Lydia was seldom seen belowstairs before eleven, and she was not the sort of person who chattered cheerfully at breakfast. Sophy returned her greeting and asked, "Have you an early engagement?"

"No, but any number of commissions. First, I must visit my modiste. Madame Dubois has sent numerous messages that she cannot complete the gowns I ordered until I arrange for the final fittings. We also have several books that must go back to the library, and I really must purchase some new gloves," Lydia said as she picked up the newspaper. "I should be pleased if you would care to join me."

"I think not," Sophy said, and hesitantly added, "I rather expect Sir George to call today."

Lydia looked up from her paper. In her agitation over Lord Blackthorn, she had completely forgotten about Sir George. "Did he say definitely that he intended to?"

"No, my dear, but I am certain he will. No doubt he will wish to discuss last evening."

Lydia made a face, preferring to forget the disastrous dinner party. "You must say all that is proper for me, then. I shall be sorry to miss him, but I really must go out. Now, do not frown, Aunt Sophy. Chances are, he will not call at all. If Lady Weymouth has her way, I am sure she will see that he is kept occupied. And I shall see him tomorrow evening when he escorts us to Lady Jersey's masquerade ball."

Sophy, knowing it was useless to argue, changed tactics. "Did you by chance see the notice in this morning's paper regarding the Duke of Lansing?"

"The announcement of his betrothal to Miss Gilbert, do you mean? I was expecting it. His Grace told me yesterday when we drove out that the notice would be in the *Gazette*."

"Imagine, Miss Gilbert will soon be a duchess. Quite a feather in her cap."

Lydia nodded. "It is, but you know Miss Gilbert does not care in the least for the title. She is sincerely attached to His Grace. I believe it will be an extremely happy marriage."

"Speaking of weddings and betrothals—" Sophy began, but Lydia interrupted her.

"May we discuss this later, Aunt Sophy? I ordered the carriage brought around, and must fly. If Sir George does call, give him my warmest regards and tell him I am looking forward to the ball."

Lydia took Finch with her, and pleased her modiste by lingering over her fittings, taking the time to look at an exquisite new silk, and ordering yet another gown. Afterward, she spent an inordinate amount of time in Oxford Street, visiting the new shop that sold every style of ladies' shoes, and an herbalist to order a fresh supply of scent. They visited Hatchard's, where Lydia purchased two new novels, and finished the afternoon by calling on Lady Granville. By four o'clock, Lydia deemed it safe to return home, and gave the order to her driver.

Pleasantly tired and pleased with her purchases, she looked forward to a soothing cup of tea, but she arrived to find the house in Bedford Square in an uproar.

Sophy, who had been on the watch for her niece, greeted her at the door. "Oh, thank heavens, you have returned! My dear, come into the drawing room. I am afraid I have dreadful news for you."

Lydia handed her packages to one of the footmen, and followed her aunt. She was not unduly alarmed, for her aunt's notions of what comprised dreadful news rarely marched with her own. But she stopped at the doorway, staring in astonishment at Lord Blackthorn, who stood near the windows.

"You did not tell me we had company," she remarked, recovering her poise.

Flustered, Sophy helplessly waved her hand. "His lordship was here when the messenger arrived from your papa, and insisted on staying—"

"A messenger from Papa?" Lydia asked, her heart suddenly sinking to her slippers.

Justin crossed the room and caught up her hand. "Yorick arrived as I drove up," he said, mentioning her father's favorite groom. "Hold tight, Liddy, 'tis bad news."

She gripped his hand, fearing the worse. "Tell me."

"Perhaps you should sit down first," Sophy suggested.

Lydia shook her head, her eyes fixed on Justin's face as she waited.

"Sir Matthew is in a coma. I am sorry, Liddy, but the doctor believes the odds are slim that he will ever recover. Your mother sent Yorick—she wishes you to come to her at once."

Lydia closed her eyes for a moment, and breathed deeply.

"Really, my lord, you might have broken the news more gently," Sophy protested.

If Lydia heard her, she gave no sign of it. Opening her eyes, she murmured, "I must go at once. Is Yorick still here? I shall need him to drive me."

"He's resting," Sophy replied. "Tomorrow, when he has sufficiently recovered, we can—"

"I cannot wait until tomorrow," Lydia interrupted, and turned to Justin. "Will you drive me home? I can be ready within the hour."

Justin nodded solemnly. "While you pack, I shall return my curricle to the stables and have a fresh team harnessed to the barouche. Don't fret, Liddy. We will make excellent time."

When she only nodded, he lifted her chin with a

touch of his gloved finger. "Sir Matthew is a fighter. There is hope yet."

"I . . . I know. I do not mean to give way."

"Good girl. In an hour, then?"

When he had gone, Sophy rounded on her niece. "I make every allowance that you are naturally overcome with grief and cannot be thinking clearly, but to consider driving to Kent in Lord Blackthorn's company goes beyond the bounds of propriety. And it will be dark in an hour. Your father would not wish—"

"Papa would wish me to reach him as soon as possible, and there is not a better whip in England than Lord Blackthorn," Lydia said as she strode toward the stairs. "Pray, excuse me, I must pack a few things, and there is not much time."

Sophy followed her up the stairs. "I cannot possibly be ready in an hour, and there are engagements we must cancel. My dear, you have not thought this through. If you will only wait until tomorrow, we can make proper traveling arrangements."

"I cannot wait, but you need not come, Aunt Sophy. I shall take Finch with me, and trust you to remain here and make whatever explanations you think suitable." She entered her bedchamber as she spoke, and her gaze instantly flew to the vanity table where the twin miniatures of her parents rested. For a moment her throat closed tightly, and a hollowness invaded her stomach. She could not bear anything to happen to her father.

Seeing the stricken look on her niece's face, Sophy placed a comforting arm about Lydia's shoulders. "My dear, I am so sorry to hear about your father. I know how much you adore him."

Lydia stepped away from her, biting her lips to keep them from trembling. She could ill afford to give in to her emotions, and an expression of sympathy was all it would take to bring the tears rushing to her eyes. She could not discuss her father—not without falling to pieces.

Turning blindly to the wardrobe, Lydia pulled several

dresses out and flung them on the bed, then curtly directed Finch to pack only what was absolutely necessary.

Sophy watched her for a moment, both hurt and puzzled by her niece's rebuff. Had she been the one to receive such news, she would have been distraught with grief, and craving the comfort of a sympathetic ear. She sighed, and knowing she was in the way, walked toward the door. She paused there. "Lydia? While I cannot approve of you traveling in this fashion, I hope you know that if there is anything I can do, you need only ask."

Her niece glanced up, and for a moment the agony she felt showed in her eyes. She spoke softly, "Thank you, Aunt Sophy. There is little any of us can do, but if you would keep Papa in your prayers?"

"Of course, my dear," Sophy assured her, then quietly left the room. She went belowstairs to the study, and sat at her desk. Regrets must be sent, she thought, and tried to formulate a list. So many people to notify . . . and, merciful heavens, what was she to say to Sir George?

Chapter 13

Beguiled by the tedium of the miles and the darkness outside the windows, Finch dozed in the carriage, but Lydia could not sleep. She thought of her father, how much he had indulged her, and how little she had given in return. She prayed silently for the opportunity to tell him how very much he was loved.

The carriage hit a deep rut, jostling the ladies inside. Finch came awake with a start, grabbing for the strap and holding on for dear life. But though she slid a little on the seat as the barouche seemed to ride on two wheels, they did not tip over. She lifted the shade at the window and peered outside. "Merciful heavens, it's as black as coal out there. His lordship will likely land us in a ditch, for how can he be seeing the road?"

"He has eyes like a cat," Lydia replied. "Rest easy, Finch. He will see us safely home."

The maid muttered to herself. She did not consider it safe to have her insides churned like buttermilk, and it was unseemly to be traveling at such a wicked pace. Lord help them if another carriage came along.

"We shall be coming into Oxford soon," Lydia said. "Lord Blackthorn will change his teams there, and then it is not so very far to Maidstone."

"Mayhap we should abide there for the night, miss. 'Tis late, and you won't be wishful of rousing the household in the dead of night—not with your papa sick and all."

"Mama will be on the lookout for me," Lydia replied implacably. "She knows I would set out at once."

"And will she be approving of your traveling in this rickety fashion with Lord Blackthorn, risking your life on a road as dark as sin?"

Lydia smiled in the darkness. "Perhaps not, Finch, but she will be as grateful to him for bringing me home as I am."

"Sir George won't approve," Finch replied darkly.

Lydia did not answer, for there was nothing she could say. She knew it would have been more prudent to wait, to send for Sir George and ask him to provide her escort. But he would have hemmed her in with his notions of propriety, insisting she travel with her aunt and her maid, a footman, outriders, and, of course, take the journey in easy stages. His coachman would never have been allowed to spring the horses and eat up the miles ...

The carriage slowed, and Lydia lifted the shade. "There are lights ahead—we must be approaching Oxford."

"The Lord be praised," Finch muttered.

Lydia watched out the window as they drove into the deserted courtyard of an inn, and a sleepy ostler stumbled out to tend the horses. Justin spoke to him for a moment, then came around the carriage and opened the door.

His dark hair was tousled from the drive, and for just an instant Lydia fancied there was a weariness in his step, but it was gone in a flash, and when he spoke it was with an air of lighthearted teasing. "So, you ladies are awake?"

"Difficult to sleep, my lord, with the carriage bouncing all over the road," Finch replied.

"Pay her no heed, Justin," Lydia advised. "My maid feels traveling in such a manner is beneath her dignity. I, however, am much obliged to you. We have made excellent time. This is Oxford, is it not?"

"It is, and you have a few moments if you wish to step inside and refresh yourself. The lad said there's a private parlor."

"I am glad of it," Lydia said as she extended her hand

and allowed him to help her down. "It will feel wonderful to walk about a little after sitting for so long."

He escorted the ladies inside, promised Liddy he would return in ten minutes, and left them in the privacy of the parlor.

"Ten minutes," Finch fumed. "Why, that is hardly time for a cup of tea, or to brush the dust from your cloak. Has his lordship no consideration for a lady's feelings?"

"He is only thinking of my desire to reach Stone's End as quickly as possible. Now, hush, Finch, or I shall begin to think I would have done better to have left you in town."

Justin returned in precisely ten minutes and found Lydia ready. He escorted her back to the carriage in silence, but as he assisted her inside, he held her hand for a moment longer than necessary, and his voice was warm with understanding as he murmured, "Not much longer now, Liddy."

"Thank you," she whispered, not trusting herself to say more.

True to his word, and despite a poorly matched team, they reached Stone's End just before two in the morning. Never had the old stone house looked so welcoming, and as Lydia has predicted, candles were burning in the lower windows.

Lady Claire had sent the servants to bed hours earlier, and it was she who came out to meet her daughter. By way of greeting, she remarked that she had expected them earlier.

"I was not at home when Yorick arrived, but I came as soon as possible," Lydia explained, and stepped into her mother's waiting arms. Neither was given to excessive displays of emotion, but for several minutes they remained locked in an embrace, each taking comfort from the other.

It was Lydia who stepped back first. Searching her mother's face, she asked, "How is Papa?"

"Much the same," Lady Claire answered. "One

161

would think he is merely sleeping, but he has not stirred or opened his eyes in two days. Tibbs is with him now and will call if there is any change. But what am I thinking of to keep you standing out here? Come inside, my dear." She turned to Justin, extending her hand. "It is good to see you again, Lord Blackthorn, and though I regret the circumstances, I must thank you for bringing my daughter home. If you will grant me a few moments, I shall have a room made ready for you."

He returned the clasp of her hand but shook his head. "I will put up at Pendenden. You will not wish to be troubled with guests, but I hope I may be permitted to call tomorrow."

"Of course, my lord." She turned tactfully to Lydia's maid. "Finch, if you will come with me, I shall show you the room Mrs. Darby has prepared in expectation of your arrival." She led the way into the house, leaving Lydia alone with Justin for a moment, a distinguishing mark of approval that was not lost on either of them.

Slightly embarrassed, Lydia extended her hand. "Thank you, Justin. I . . . I know it was audacious of me to have asked for your help, and no doubt you must think it strange that I did not send for Sir George, but—"

"Not in the least, Liddy. You forget that I have seen him drive. You would have been days on the road."

She smiled dutifully, but remained serious as she tried to explain her feelings. "You are being kind, Justin, and I do not deserve that after the hateful things I have said to you."

"Egad, is this an apology, Liddy? You must be more tired than I thought." Before she knew what he was about, Justin dropped a swift kiss on her brow, then turned her toward the house. "Go to bed, sweetheart. And do not be imagining yourself indebted to me. I am fond of Sir Matthew and would have come even had you not asked."

She was tired, unbearably so. She allowed him to usher her into the hall, then lingered for a moment, watching as he strode toward his carriage. He might be arrogant, high-handed, and opinionated, but she was suddenly very glad he'd come home with her.

Finch had her nightclothes laid out and the bed turned down, but Lydia could not retire until she'd seen her father. She tiptoed quietly down the hall and found her mother waiting for her outside their bedchamber.

"I knew you would wish to see him," Lady Claire said softly, and held out her hand. Together, they walked silently into the room and approached the four-poster.

Lydia looked down at her papa. He'd always been a vibrant man, full of life, never able to sit still for long. His booming voice had echoed in the halls of Stone's End for as long as she could remember. He looked smaller now, and to see him lying so still, so defenseless, brought tears to her eyes.

Her mother placed a comforting arm about her shoulders. "Dr. Longfellow said he is in no pain."

Lydia nodded, then stooped and placed a kiss on her father's leathery cheek. "Sweet dreams, Papa," she said as she had done so many times as a little girl.

For three days, Lydia kept a vigil beside her father's bed, sharing the nursing duties with her mother and Tibbs, the valet who'd served Sir Matthew since Lydia was a toddler. She left her father's side only to eat or sleep, except for the hour or two each day when Justin called and persuaded her to walk in the garden. He was with her on Monday after she had talked to the doctor.

"I cannot believe that there is nothing we can do for Papa, except wait," she complained, not for the first time.

"I know 'tis difficult. Have you tried talking to him?"

She glanced up at him as though he'd lost his mind, and answered sadly, "I would give the world to do so, but Papa is in a coma, Justin. He cannot see, or hear, or feel."

"Maybe, but the doctors are not certain of that. I was

thinking about John Fairington, a young man in my regiment. When we were in Spain, he took a nasty blow to the head, and like Sir Matthew went into a coma. The doctor did not offer much hope, but there was a young Spanish girl who had become much attached to him, and it was she who nursed him. There were many who thought she was foolish, but she talked to him continuously, and one night Fairington answered her. He recovered swiftly after that."

"And you think it was because she talked to him?"

Justin shrugged, not wanting to raise her hopes too high. "Who knows, Liddy? He may have regained consciousness had she done nothing, but he was convinced she had saved his life."

"I will try it, then," she said wearily.

"I wish I could offer more help, both for Sir Matthew's sake and your own. I hate to see you looking so pale, and I know you must be exhausted. You have not argued with me once in the past three days."

She laughed at that. "But you have done nothing to which I could take exception. Indeed, I am conscious of how much I stand in your debt—"

"None of that," he interrupted as he turned their steps toward the house. "Lord, to think I once believed that if you ever ceased railing at me, I would be the happiest man in England. How ironic now to find that I rather miss that sharp tongue of yours."

"If that was intended as a compliment, my lord, it falls short of the mark. Obviously there is no pleasing you, for you do not know what it is you want."

They had reached the terrace, and he paused beside the long casement windows that led inside. Gazing tenderly down at her, he brushed her cheek with the tip of his finger. "I know, Liddy. I have known for five years."

"Justin, please, I—"

He placed his finger over her lips. "Hush. I should not have spoken yet. I know you can think of nothing now except Sir Matthew. I shall see you tomorrow."

He left her before she could protest, and Lydia slowly walked inside. She was too tired to think clearly, too confused to know her own mind. She climbed the stairs, and tapped softly on her father's bedchamber door.

Lady Claire bid her enter, and Lydia joined her, taking one of the chairs drawn up to the side of the large four-poster bed. She told her mother what Justin had said. Lady Claire agreed it was worth trying, and she and Lydia took turns throughout the long afternoon and evening. They spoke to him of family matters, of the estate and the tenants, and read to him from the Bible.

Nothing seemed to have any effect, but Lady Claire said it comforted her to talk to him, and she would continue to try. She urged Lydia to try to sleep, and promised to wake her daughter at two o'clock, when she herself would rest awhile.

Lydia obeyed, but it seemed as though she had barely closed her eyes when her mother roused her. She opened sleepy eyes to gaze into her mother's face, and it took her a moment to realize Lady Claire was smiling.

"Mama, what—"

"Come quickly, darling. Your father is awake and asking for you. I do not want to place too much dependence on it, but he seems much like his old self. I have sent Yorick for Dr. Longfellow, but, oh, my dear, is it not wonderful?"

Lydia agreed it was and slipped from the bed. She hurriedly pulled on a wrapper and followed her mother down the long hall. "How did it happen?"

"I was sitting beside him, holding his hand, and telling him how much we missed him, and I suddenly felt his fingers respond to mine. I thought at first that it was my imagination, but then he opened his eyes."

Lydia squeezed her hand as they walked into the bedchamber. Sir Matthew was propped up against the pillows, his eyes shut, and for a moment Lydia feared he had lapsed back into a coma. But as she approached the bed, she saw his hand twitch against the covers.

"Papa?" she whispered softly as she sat on the edge of the bed. "Papa, it is Lydia."

His eyes opened slowly and traveled over her face. "Lydia. Dreamed ... you were here." His voice was hoarse, the words slurred, and his eyes fluttered shut again. But there was warmth in the hand she gripped, and her hot tears fell against his cheek.

"Papa, oh, Papa, don't leave us again."

"Thirsty," he muttered, and turned restlessly.

Lady Claire quickly poured a glass of water from the pitcher on the bedside table. Between her and Lydia, they held him up so that he could sip from the glass.

"Do not let him drink too much," Lady Claire warned. "Not until Dr. Longfellow has seen him and can advise us. I do wish he would hurry."

Her warning was unnecessary. Sir Matthew swallowed only a sip or two before once again closing his eyes. He slept, but not in the still, frightening way of a coma. His hand remained clasped in his wife's, his fingers curling weakly against hers, and he occasionally moaned in his sleep.

Dr. Longfellow was admitted thirty minutes later. He was able to rouse Sir Matthew for a few moments, professed himself pleased to see that his patient recognized him, and nodded to himself from time to time. When he was done with his examination, he spoke to Lady Claire and Lydia in the hall.

"A most remarkable recovery, and I believe he is out of danger now, though the next few days will be critical—and difficult for someone of Sir Matthew's temperament. He will be weak at first, which will annoy him. You may allow him to get up a little each day, but do not permit him to overtax himself. His strength will return slowly. For the first few days, feed him nourishing broths." He chuckled and added, "When he threatens to throw the bowl at you, allow him a bit of chicken or fish. Send for me if anything occurs to alarm you, but I do not anticipate it. Just keep him quiet, and keep any news from him that is likely to excite him. His

166

heart is still a little weak, but I expect in a few weeks, he will be his old self."

With the crisis over, Lydia's strength seemed to drain from her. It was close to three when she finally crawled into bed, and she fell into a deep, dreamless sleep. Lady Claire looked in on her once, and left orders that her daughter was not to be disturbed.

As a consequence, it was after ten when Lydia awoke the next morning. The first thing she noticed was the fresh breeze wafting in the open windows, and drowsily thought how sweet the air was in Kent. Rubbing the sleep from her eyes, she stretched, and then wondered what time it was. Papa! Memories of the night before came rushing back, and she was eager to see him again to make certain it had not been just a dream. Why had no one called her? The sun was well up. She flung back the cover, intending to ring for her maid, but before she could, Finch quietly opened the door and glanced in.

"Morning, miss. I thought you might be stirring by now. I brought your chocolate up."

"Why the devil didn't you wake me sooner?" Lydia demanded.

"Because Lady Claire gave orders you were not to be disturbed, and your papa is doing just fine, so don't be fretting yourself."

"Oh. Well, thank you, Finch," Lydia said, reclining against the pillows. She took a sip of the hot chocolate and sighed. She had not enjoyed the luxury of a morning in bed for several days, and it was lovely, but guilt nibbled at her conscience. "Are you certain Papa is well? Is Mama with him?"

"She is, and I just spoke to Tibbs, what waits on him. He said as how Sir Matthew is already complaining at being served gruel for breakfast."

"Then, he *is* on the mend," Lydia said smiling happily.

"I'd say so, miss, and Lady Claire said to tell you that she sent word to Lord Blackthorn letting him know, so you need not be worrying about that neither. She said after you get dressed, you can come talk to your papa."

Feeling as though a weight had been lifted from her shoulders, Lydia took her time over her morning toilet. She chose to wear a pretty sprig muslin gown that she'd left behind on her last visit. Its lines were too simple for London, but perfect for a summer day in the country. Her hair was brushed back and caught with a green ribbon, so that it fell in soft curls to her shoulders. She looked as lighthearted as she felt, and hummed as she walked down the hall to her father's bedchamber.

Tibbs admitted her, and she thought she'd never seen a more welcome sight than her papa, sitting up in bed, his green eyes gazing at her fondly.

"About time you came home," he growled. "Come give your poor old da a kiss."

She did so, then sat on the bed, holding his hand. He was thinner, his lips looked painfully cracked, and the fingers gripping hers were not as strong as they once were. Still, his eyes were clear and bright. She smiled down at him. "I am so glad to see you looking so much better, Papa. You gave Mama and me a terrible fright."

"I'll not regret it, not if that is what it takes to bring my little girl home for a visit. 'Tis been too long since we've seen you, Lydia. I worry about you in London, with no husband to look after you."

"Well, you need not. I am fine, Papa, as you can see. And the next time you are wishful of my company, please just send me a letter. I promise I will—"

Her father suffered a fit of coughing, his face turning red as he tried to get his breath. Tibbs was beside him in an instant, supporting his shoulders so he could sip from a glass of water, then lowering him to rest against the pillows. Lydia watched as her father closed his eyes, fear squeezing her heart as she realized he was still far from well.

He rested quietly, but she could hear the raspy sound of his breathing. They were going to have to tread carefully, she thought. She remained beside him for a quarter hour, holding his hand, until it seemed he was asleep. But, when she stood up, he opened his eyes again. "Lydia?"

"What is it, Papa?" she asked, smiling tenderly at him even while her heart ached.

"Your mother . . . said . . . Justin brought you home."

"He did, and he will be wishful of looking in on you, himself. He has called every day."

"He's a good lad . . . marry him, Liddy."

She stared at him in astonishment. "But, Papa, I—"

"Obey me, Liddy, just once . . . it will ease my mind to know you are safely wed." His hand clutched at his chest as though he were in terrible pain, and he closed his eyes for a moment. "Promise me," he gasped, clinging to her hand.

She nodded helplessly. "If you wish it, Papa. Now, please try to rest. We can talk of this later."

"Bring him . . . bring Justin to see me," Sir Matthew ordered weakly. Then his eyes closed again, and his head lolled against the pillows.

"He'll sleep now, miss," Tibbs said, adjusting the pillows, and pulling the cover up about Sir Matthew.

Lydia barely heard him. She fled the room, seeking a few moments' privacy, but encountered her mother in the hall. Her stricken face told its own story.

"Darling, what is wrong?" Lady Claire cried. "Not—not your father?"

"No, he is sleeping," Lydia quickly assured her. "But, oh, Mama, he wants . . . he wants me to marry Justin. I did not know what to say. Papa could not get his breath, and he looked so ill. He said he worries about me, and he made me promise I would wed Justin. What am I going to do?"

Lady Claire hugged her daughter. "It must have been preying on his mind. Darling, he worries that you have never wed. He spoke of it often these last few months. You know he never gave up hope that you and Lord Blackthorn would make a match of it, and since you

169

had not formed an attachment to anyone else, he still cherishes that hope."

"But that's just it, Mama. I have formed an attachment—it is all but settled. Oh, Sir George has not asked me yet, but I have met his family, and I was going to invite him to come down to meet you and Papa."

"I see," Lady Claire said, her slim brows rising. "I must confess that when Lord Blackthorn drove you home, I thought the two of you had arrived at an understanding, but if that is not the case . . . oh, my dear, I do not know what to advise."

"I shall have to tell Papa the truth," Lydia declared. "I am sure that once I explain about Sir George, Papa will understand."

"Perhaps, but—darling, I do not like to ask it of you—but could you not delay? Dr. Longfellow said your father must not be excited just now. If it soothes him to think that you have agreed to wed Lord Blackthorn, could we not allow him to believe it, just until he recovers his strength?"

"Mama!"

"I am only thinking of your father, Lydia. Surely it could do no harm to postpone telling him the truth for a week or two. Just until he gets his strength back," Lady Claire coaxed.

Lydia sighed. "I do not know what is best. He wishes to see Justin."

"Then, I pray you will arrange it. Your papa must not be vexed just now, Lydia. Lord Blackthorn is a fine gentleman, and extremely fond of Sir Matthew. I am certain that if you explain the situation, he will wish to do all possible to help. And we need only maintain the fiction for a few days . . . just until your papa regains his strength.

Chapter 14

When Justin called that afternoon, Lydia received him in the blue drawing room. He came toward her with hands outstretched and a wide grin. "Liddy, what splendid news! I received word from Lady Claire that your father is out of the coma and on the mend. I can guess how delighted you must be."

"Indeed, although we are not out of the woods yet. The next few days are critical, but if we can contrive to keep Papa quiet, Dr. Longfellow believes he will completely recover. Do sit down, Justin. There is something I must discuss with you."

Puzzled, he took the chair she indicated. He had expected to find her in high spirits. Instead there was a troubled look in her green eyes that worried him. "What is it, Liddy? I can see something is disturbing you."

"I never could keep any secrets from you," she said, and poured a cup of tea for both of them.

"Nor had any reason to," he said. "At least I hope not. I always thought we could discuss most any topic—even if it were only to disagree. I beg you will not hide your teeth with me now."

She smiled, but found it more difficult than she had imagined to broach her problem. She took a sip of the tea. "I am concerned about Papa, Justin. You know that he has always wished that we . . . that we would wed?"

Justin grinned. "He has told me so on any number of occasions. Surely that comes as no surprise to you?"

"No, but—well, he has this idiotic notion in his head. Mama told him that you drove me home, and I am afraid that he assumed that we, that is, that you and I had—" she broke off her words, a deep blush stealing up her cheeks.

"He thinks we patched up our quarrel, is that it?" Justin asked, amusement lighting his eyes. "Well, what is there in that to overset you? 'Tis nearly the truth. We have not quarreled in several days."

She took a deep breath. Her father had always advised her to get over rough ground as quickly as possible. Avoiding Justin's gaze, she said, "He asked that I give him my promise to wed you."

Justin set his cup down. He had a notion that he was beginning to understand Lydia's dilemma, and fond as he was of Sir Matthew, at that moment he did not think kindly of him for his interference. He said quietly, "I very much wish he had not done that."

"As do I! But he is not yet well, and Mama thinks it inadvisable to argue with him. She fears that if I gainsay him now, he might lapse back into a coma."

"Am I to gather, then, that you gave him your promise?" A wry smile curved the corners of his mouth, but his eyes were unreadable, and his voice carried a sharp sting. "Should I now consider myself betrothed? When are we to discuss the marriage settlements?"

She stretched out a hand. "Justin, I am terribly sorry. I realize this places you in an intolerable position, and you must believe I never would have agreed had not Papa been so ill. I did try to explain, but he had some sort of attack and could not get his breath. I feared to argue with him further. You do understand, do you not?"

"Unfortunately I do."

She wished she knew what he was thinking. He was not angry, not precisely, nor was he pleased. Of course, she could not blame him. Looking down at her hands, she said, "Mama thought if we could merely delay telling him the truth for a few days, just until he is stronger, that it would ease his mind. I hate to ask you to be

172

a part of such a deception, but for Papa's sake, would you be willing?"

Save for the ticking of the mantel clock, there was silence in the room. Nervously Lydia glanced up.

She watched Justin as he rose and strode toward the windows. For a moment, she thought he intended to leave without a word. But when he remained standing there, his back rigid, silently staring out at the gardens, she went to him. Laying a gentle hand on his arm, she said, "I know such deceit is abhorrent to you, but I felt there was no other choice."

"There is one alternative," he replied as he turned and glanced down at her. "We could make it official."

Her chin came up, and a flare of pride flashed in her eyes. "I will not allow my father to force us into such an arrangement. It may be necessary to accede to his wishes for the moment, but I assure you that as soon as he is well enough to stand the shock, I shall tell him the truth."

"I rather thought you would say that," Justin replied. "Very well, let us get this travesty over with. Does he wish to see me now? Lead the way."

"If you will wait here, I shall see if he is awake," Lydia said, but something in Justin's manner alarmed her. There was an air of recklessness about him, and an underlying anger. She supposed it was only natural, and she could understand his frustration, but if he faced her father in such a mood, Sir Matthew would never believe that they were happily betrothed.

Troubled, she went up to her father's room. She half hoped he would be sleeping, but he was awake, and when she told him her errand, he announced himself ready to meet with his future son-in-law.

"Now, Papa," she cautioned, "there will be ample time to arrange the settlements and such when you are feeling better. I beg you will not tax yourself, and I've warned Justin that he may visit only for a few moments."

"Believe me, daughter, nothing will restore me to

health quicker than knowing you will be cared for. Send Justin to me, and do not worry your pretty head."

Reluctantly Lydia left and returned a few moments later with Justin. Before they entered the room, she begged him to remember that her father was not well. She showed him in, and would have stayed, but neither man would agree to her remaining in the room. Lydia nervously paced the hall outside until a quarter hour had passed. Then she marched resolutely to the door, and opened it.

Justin was seated by the bed, turned away from her. Her father, propped up against several pillows, looked much improved, and smiled at her. "Come in, my dear, come in. I was just about to send for you."

"Were you, Papa? I did not mean to intrude, but Dr. Longfellow said your visits must of necessity be kept short. I believe you should rest now."

Justin had risen at her entrance, and held out a hand to her. "Come here, my sweet. You need not be worried. Sir Matthew and I have reached an amicable settlement."

Aware her father was watching, she reluctantly gave Justin her hand, and tried to summon a smile.

"I believe it is customary to seal such a bargain," he murmured, and pulled her into a close embrace.

"That a boy," Sir Matthew crowed. "Buss her one."

Color flamed in her face as Justin willingly obliged. His arms held her captive as his lips claimed hers, rousing old memories and old passions. Despite her father watching, despite her own reluctance, her body responded with a will of its own. Her eyes closed, and her hands caressed the broad expanse of his back as her lips willingly answered his. Desire flamed within her, burning away any remnants of decency and propriety.

Justin abruptly released her, and the knowing look in his blue eyes as he gazed down at her, filled her with mortification.

"Signed, sealed, and delivered," Sir Matthew chortled. "Children, you have made me very happy."

Struggling to regain her composure, Lydia walked toward the door. "I believe you have had enough excitement for one day, Papa. We will leave you to rest now. Justin, I would have a word with you before you leave. Would you join me in the drawing room?"

She rounded on him the moment the doors were shut. "I do not find your conduct amusing, sir."

He grinned. "Not amusing, but confess you enjoyed sealing our betrothal as much as I did."

Ignoring that, she retorted, "Need I remind you that we are not truly betrothed?"

He shrugged. "Sir Matthew expected nothing less. He would not have believed in our little charade otherwise. I was only trying to oblige you, Liddy."

She shot a dagger look at him. "How kind of you, but I trust you will not be tempted to repeat such a performance. Papa appears to be much better, and it cannot be above a day or two before we can tell him the truth."

Ten days later, Lydia sat at the breakfast table, fuming. "Mama, I do not know what to do. Every time I attempt to tell Papa that Justin and I are not betrothed, he has another one of those attacks."

Lady Claire sighed. "It is difficult to know what to suggest, my dear. Is Lord Blackthorn growing impatient?"

Lydia sighed. "No, he is willing to continue this deception as long as necessary, but each day we delay, it becomes more complicated. Papa told both Dr. Longfellow and Squire Berkley of our betrothal, and when I went into the village yesterday, Mrs. Melrose asked me when the wedding would be. The longer we delay, the more difficult it is going to be to explain to everyone."

"What does Lord Blackthorn advise?"

She made a face. "Justin feels that when the time comes, we can give it out that I jilted him." She did not care to mention that he had remarked that inasmuch as she had done so before, it would not come as any great surprise to anyone if she left him at the altar again.

Lydia had naturally pointed out that it was he who had broken their troth, but her heart was not in the argument. The fact that he had once chosen his duty to the military over his commitment to her no longer seemed quite so reprehensible an act as it once had.

She found it impossible to remain angry with him, especially since he was behaving so generously in the matter of their supposed engagement. Far from being impatient, Justin took pains to ensure that Sir Matthew would suspect nothing. He called every day, took her driving several times, and had even escorted her to dinner at the squire's—and behaved like a perfect gentleman.

Lydia had feared that their ambiguous situation might tempt him to try to repeat the kiss he'd claimed. She was fully prepared to put him in his place if he did, but he never strayed beyond the line. Not even when he'd driven her home from the squire's.

The night had been balmy, the velvet sky crowded with an abundance of stars, and the moonlit courtyard deserted. Justin had strolled with her to the door. Lydia remembered how she'd shivered in anticipation . . . not that she wanted him to kiss her, but she had thought he intended to. He had taken her hand, and murmured, "I feel as though the clock has been turned back. Did we not stand here after a dinner at the squire's five years ago?"

She laughed, hoping to break the tension between them. "We did, and if I recollect correctly, even the same guests were present. Mrs. Melrose, and Caroline Cathcart, the Havershams, and—"

"There is only one thing I remember about that evening," Justin interrupted softly, "and it was not the guest list."

He stood tantalizingly close. She knew if she looked up, his mouth would be but inches from hers.

"That was the night I proposed to you."

Her heart racing furiously, she stood perfectly still. He had kissed her that night, kissed her until her lips were bruised, and then kissed her again with a tenderness that had made her heart ache. Foolish desires surged within her.

Justin stepped away from her, and laughed lightly. "At least I need not make that mistake again. Good night, Liddy."

She'd felt like a fool.

"Lydia?"

Her mother's voice brought her sharply back to the present. Annoyed with herself, she sipped her tea and tried to appear composed. But she quickly forgot her own feelings as she noticed her mother's puzzled expression. "What is it, Mama?"

Lady Claire was sorting through the morning post and the number of letters she set aside for her daughter were growing into a tidy stack. "Gracious, have you been spending all your time writing to friends? I cannot recall you ever receiving so much correspondence except when—well, it has been a good many years."

Except when your engagement was announced.

The unspoken words hung between them. Lydia hated writing letters as much as her mother did, and as a consequence received few. During the past week, she had thought several times of writing to Aunt Sophy and Sir George, but she had not known quite what to say, and put it off. She had not even written to Perdita.

"I suppose my friends are becoming worried at my silence," Lydia said as her mother passed a number of the envelopes to her. She recognized Perdita's delicate script, and opened that one first. Lydia read a few lines, then let the letter fall, the color draining from her face. Too angry to speak, she handed her mother the letter.

"Darling, is it bad news?"

"Read it!" Lydia ordered, her mouth pressed into a grim line, and her foot tapping ominously.

"Dearest Lydia," Lady Claire read aloud. "I do not know if I shall ever forgive you, or Justin. To think that

177

I had to learn of my dearest friend's engagement to my own brother from the *Gazette*. I could not believe my eyes when I saw the announcement this morning."

Lady Claire quietly laid down the page, resigned to the storm ahead. "Lydia, my dear, I am sorry. I am responsible for this—"

"Mama, you will never convince me that you put that notice in the *Gazette*."

"No, not that, but I fear I am responsible for it all the same. I am the one who persuaded you to deceive your father, and this is what comes of it. He sent for James last week—that young man who handles all his business affairs—perhaps I should have suspected, but it never occurred to me that Matthew would think to send an announcement out. My dear, I am so terribly sorry."

"Not as sorry as Papa is going to be," Lydia declared, fire in her eyes.

"I realize you are angry, and with reason, but you cannot—you must not—reproach your father. My dear, do try to think this through sensibly. Even if your father were well, there could be no point in taking him to task. He only did what he thought was proper."

"Did he, Mama? Or did he think to tie me irrevocably to Justin? Our betrothal was not announced five years ago, because Justin would not permit it, not until he was certain he would return safely. Perhaps Papa thought that publishing the announcement would make it more difficult for me, should I choose to withdraw."

"And if he did, would that be so wrong of him?" Lady Claire demanded. "He is your father, Lydia, and naturally must wish to see you safely wed. If, the good Lord forbid, something should happen to him, you would be alone in the world."

Before Lydia could think of a suitable reply, the butler tapped on the door, then stepped into the room. "Begging your pardon, Lady Claire, but Miss Remfrey has arrived from London and is wishful of a word with Miss Lydia."

"Aunt Sophy! Oh, good heavens. Edwards, please

show her into the drawing room, and tell her I shall be with her directly," Lydia ordered as she rose.

"No doubt Sophia will wish to stay the night. I shall have Mrs. Darby prepare a room, and then join you," Lady Claire said as she, too, rose. "Oh, dear, I suppose she saw the announcement."

"I am certain of it. What am I to tell her, Mama?"

"She is family, Lydia. I suggest you tell her the truth and ask her to keep your confidence. I am sure Sophia will understand."

Lydia took a deep, calming breath, summoned a smile, and went to greet her aunt. Her first impression was that Sophy was looking remarkably well. Perhaps it was the journey and the fresh air, but Lydia fancied there was a sparkle in her aunt's eyes, and a becoming color in her cheeks that she had never noticed previously.

The two ladies hugged, and then Sophy stepped back. "I am sure you must be wondering why I have come."

"I fear I have a very good notion, Aunt Sophy, and really must apologize for not writing to you. I certainly intended to, but—"

"I quite understand, my dear, and there is not the least reason for an apology, unless it is the one that I owe you."

"For turning up unexpectedly? Do not be silly, Aunt Sophy. Mama was just saying how pleasant it will be to see you again, and is having a room prepared for you. She will join us in a moment or two."

The door opened and Lydia glanced around, expecting to see her mother, but it was the butler again. "Pardon, Miss Lydia, but Lord Blackthorn insists—"

"No need for such formality," Justin interrupted, strolling into the room. "After all, as Miss Lydia's intended, I am nearly family."

"Really, Justin," Lydia remonstrated. "Did Edwards not tell you that my aunt has just arrived from London? I have barely exchanged a word with her."

"Ah, Miss Remfrey," Justin said, executing a neat

bow. "Your servant, ma'am. Did you drive down to inquire about Sir Matthew?"

"No, my lord, though in light of the announcement I saw in the paper, I trust he is on the road to recovery. I, however, came to discuss a very personal—and private—matter with Lydia. Perhaps you would be so good as to leave us for a few moments?"

"How coincidental, Miss Remfrey. I, too, have a most urgent matter I must discuss with Lydia. Shall we draw straws for the privilege?"

The door opened again to admit Lady Claire. "Well, this is a pleasant surprise. Sophia, how delightful to see you again, and Lord Blackthorn, you are abroad early."

"I fear there is a matter of some urgency that I must discuss with your daughter," Justin murmured.

"Oh? I see, well—"

"I, too, must speak with Lydia," Sophy protested.

The doors swung open again and Sir Matthew, assisted by his valet, walked into the room. "Well, now. My first day belowstairs, and the family is all gathered."

"Matthew, are you well enough to be out of bed?" Lady Claire asked, going at once to his side.

"Papa! I am so glad to see you so much recovered. There is something I must say to you."

"Not now," Justin warned, coming up behind her. "Liddy, I must speak with you alone, and at once. Please step into the garden with me."

"Have you lost your mind?" she hissed.

"Very nearly, and I am warning you—if you do not come willingly, I shall carry you out."

"You would not dare," she whispered, but the look in his eyes warned her that he would. She turned around, hoping she did not appear as beset as she felt. "Aunt Sophy, Mama, Papa, would you pray excuse us for a few moments? I promise you, I shall not be long."

"Take your time, daughter," Sir Matthew boomed. "I recollect how it was to be young. So, Sophy, what brings you down from London?"

Lydia did not hear her reply. Yielding to the insistent tug on her arm, she followed Justin out to the garden. Once beyond the terrace, she wheeled and furiously confronted him. "What the devil is the matter with you?"

"I wanted to talk to you before you spoke with your aunt. I had a letter from Perdita this morning."

"She wrote me, also, and if this is about the announcement in the *Gazette*, I am very sorry. I know it will be embarrassing, but you need not fear I will hold you to it."

"I never feared that, Liddy. Did Perdita perchance mention Sir George?"

Lydia shrugged. "She may have. To be honest, I did not finish her letter, nor have I yet read the dozens of others I received. I . . . I suppose he is hurt. I should have written to him. No doubt that is what my aunt wishes to speak to me about. She has always been very fond of Sir George, and must be thinking me quite heartless."

"So you intend to tell her our engagement is a sham?"

She nodded. "This farce has gone on long enough. But you need not fear it will be spread all over town. I am certain Aunt Sophy will keep our confidence."

"I see. And your father?"

Lydia sighed. "Telling him the truth will be the most difficult of all, but I believe he is certainly well enough now to stand the shock. As soon as I can speak to him privately, I will tell him the truth."

"That will settle it, then?" he asked in a peculiar voice. "You will not feel obliged to marry me, not for your father's sake, or because of the gossip?"

"Certainly not. We have weathered gossip before—"

"Good. Allow me one more, possibly, two more questions, and then I shall allow you to return to the house. First, what do you intend to do about Sir George?"

"Perhaps you should have been a barrister, my lord.

This is beginning to feel like an inquisition. I do not see what concern it is of yours."

"I have a very good reason for asking, Liddy. Do you still intend to wed him?"

She turned away from his piercing eyes and plucked a rose, unconsciously shredding the velvety petals. "If you must know, I ... I have decided that we will not suit. I was going to write to him." She laughed, mocking herself. "My affairs have turned out wretchedly, but at least Lady Weymouth will be pleased."

"She is not the only one," Justin replied. He placed his hands on her shoulders and gently turned her to face him. "One more question, my sweet."

Butterflies swarmed in her stomach, and she suddenly found it difficult to get her breath. Nor could she look at him.

Justin placed a finger beneath her chin, and gently lifted. His gaze was tender, his voice solemn, as he asked, "Miss Osborne, will you do me the honor of becoming my wife?"

Sudden tears misted her eyes, but she blinked them back. "I do not know what to say," she whispered.

He laughed. "Lord, Liddy, you cannot claim 'tis sudden." Without warning, he drew her into his embrace, his arms tightening like steel bands around her. "I have loved you forever," he murmured softly as his mouth captured hers. He lengthened the kiss, deepened it, until she responded and he felt her hands about his shoulders and her slender body willingly surrender to his.

He lifted his head to brush a tender kiss against her temple, where he could feel her pulse beating rapidly, and at the corner of her lips.

"Not forever," she whispered against his mouth. "Only five years."

He grinned. "It seems like forever, my sweet, and I pledge you it will be. If you will have me, I am forever yours."

"Why did you wait so long?" she asked, knowing she was treading on dangerous ground. But the only punishment she received was another kiss that left her too breathless to argue.

It was several moments before either noticed Finch standing in the path at the curve of the garden. She was smiling in pleased approval when Justin spotted her, but she quickly assumed an innocent demeanor, bobbed a curtsy, and said, "Pardon me, Miss Lydia, but Lady Claire sent me to find you. Your aunt Sophy is waiting to see you."

"Tell her you saw no sign of us," Justin suggested.

Lydia hushed him. "I shall be in in a moment, Finch. Thank you." Flushed, disheveled, and impossibly happy, she stood on tiptoe and kissed Justin's cheek. "I have but one stipulation, my lord. I wish to be wed in six months' time. I have no intention of waiting a year."

"I was thinking more like three months," he said. "We've wasted too much time as it is."

Lady Claire was about to send Finch to search for her daughter again, when Lydia and Justin entered the drawing room, hand in hand. Sir Matthew looked a question at his future son-in-law, and received a brief nod and smile in return. He chortled happily, poked his wife in the ribs, and whispered, "I knew all they needed was a nudge. 'Tis settled now."

Lydia left Justin by the door, and approached her aunt, holding out her hand. "Aunt Sophy, I must apologize for keeping you waiting. If you will come with me—"

The door swung open and Edwards stepped in, looking harassed. "I beg your pardon, my lady, my lords, but Sir George Weymouth has called and insists on seeing Miss Lydia and Miss Remfrey at once."

Sophy rose from her chair. "Sir George here? I—"

"What the devil does that fellow want here? Didn't he see the announcement?" Sir Matthew boomed while Lady Claire tried to hush him.

"I suggest you show Sir George in," Justin said as he

leaned against the fireplace mantel, looking much amused.

"Miss Lambert is also here, my lord, and Mr. Richmond."

"What?" Sir Matthew demanded. "Who's Richmond and what business has he here? Miss Lambert is family, but I don't know any Richmond."

"Show them all in," Justin advised, and held out a hand to Lydia. "Scared?" he asked quietly as she joined him.

She shook her head. "Embarrassed, and sorry to hurt Sir George in this way—but I cannot regret it."

They all came in at once. Ignoring the others, Sir George went straight to Sophy. "My dear, I came as soon as I received your note." He tucked her hand in his arm and turned to face Lydia. "Your aunt feels we owe you the extraordinary civility of an explanation. I do not, considering your conduct, but I honor her wishes."

"I do not understand," Lydia said, looking in confusion at the pair before her.

Sophy's face flamed, and she stammered. "I—I wanted to tell you privately, my dear, to explain . . . Sir George has asked me to be his wife."

Lydia stared at her for a moment in astonishment, then laughed. "Oh, how wonderful. Aunt Sophy, I could not be happier for you."

"Then, you are not angry—"

"How could I be? Indeed, I think you perfectly suited."

"Well, now, fancy that," Sir Matthew boomed. "Puts a different complexion on things, don't it? I believe this calls for a toast—except, who is that fellow?"

Justin stepped forward. "May I present my future brother-in-law? Sir Matthew, Cedric Richmond."

"Richmond is it? You've the look of the military about you."

"Yes, sir. I served under Lord Blackthorn—"

"Capital. I shall wish to hear all about it. Claire?

184